Devil's Work

Margaret Yorke

Devil's Work

St. Martin's Press
New York

FINW -1

Yorke, Margaret.
  Devil's work.

  I. Title.
PR6075.07D4   1982   823'.914   82-5614
ISBN 0-312-19867-1   AACR2

First published in London by Hutchinson & Co., Ltd.
First U.S. Edition

10 9 8 7 6 5 4 3 2 1   C\

Hell is paved with good intentions and roofed with lost opportunities.

Unknown (Portuguese)

It is easy – terribly easy – to shake a man's faith in himself. To take advantage of that to break a man's spirit is devil's work.

Bernard Shaw, *Candida*

1

The house was empty.

The child stared at the dull brick front, studded with blank, uncurtained windows under a gabled roof; at the closed front door with its familiar dark green paint. She rang the bell again and again, and, when still no one came, thumped the heavy brass knocker, hearing the sound echo through the deserted building. In a frenzy of terror she pushed open the shining brass letter-box flap and peered through, seeing bare, scratched floorboards which, that morning when she left for school, had been covered with dark brown haircord carpeting stretching the length of the hall to the kitchen door. She could see on the walls the patterned paper she had known all her life, but now, where a watercolour painting of a ship in full sail had hung, there was a large, lighter square patch. A coat rack had stood at the foot of the stairs and on it, each afternoon, she had hung her coat and her round felt hat. Later, her father would hang his herringbone tweed overcoat next to hers, and the hat he wore to the office, placing his rolled umbrella in the tub nearby. He would slick down his hair with a brush kept handy on a shelf at the side of the coat rack, frowning at himself in a small mirror above it as he did so, before going into the living-room with the evening paper.

She could see the stairs rising steeply at the back of the hall. They had been covered with a patterned carpet in greens and browns which, in her solitary games, she had pretended was a jungle path covered with creeper-like growth that hid lizards and menacing beasts. Now the carpet was gone, and the treads climbed nakedly upwards to what must be equal desolation on the upper floors, where at the top was her own small room, with its narrow bed, her dolls, and a few books.

Her mother should be in the kitchen preparing tea: hot dripping toast if her mood was good, or even scones, but at least bread and jam, with the light on and the house warm.

But there was no one, and it was nearly dark.

Standing on the doorstep, she began to scream.

2

On a Monday in February, Alan Parker drove eastwards through Berbridge's morning rush hour. Slowing for traffic lights, he noticed a blue Ford Fiesta at a side road, its driver waiting for a gap in the passing stream of cars so that it could emerge. Alan, a patient man, tried every day to make some other road user happy by yielding way when it was not mandatory; he stopped and signalled to the Fiesta's driver, a young woman, to move. The car was full of children, he saw, as she waved her thanks and entered the main road.

Moving up behind the blue car, Alan saw several small heads inside; one child climbed up on the rear seat to look at him through the window, grinning and waving as the traffic lights turned to green. Alan waved back, but then the child's face disappeared as he was told, no doubt, to turn round and sit still.

They went on in convoy, and after half a mile or so the Fiesta's driver indicated her intention to turn off. Alan, bound for the city centre, turned too, and followed the Fiesta down a residential street where he had not been for years. On one side were semidetached houses, fifty or sixty years old, their small front gardens separated from the pavement by low walls backed with iron railings. On the other side the houses were larger, and detached. After some distance, newer houses could be seen; they were built in groups inserted where older dwellings had been demolished, and still further on there was a modern shopping centre with a row of shops set back from the road behind a wide pavement.

Alan scarcely recognized the area. There had been a cinema here, he recalled, the Plaza, and some quite different shops. Now that he thought about it, there had been controversy as to how the district should be developed when the cinema was sold.

The Fiesta turned left beyond the shops, continued for a short distance along the road, and then pulled in at the kerb. The nearside door opened and the small passengers clambered out. Other children were getting out of more cars, and there was a stream of mothers, some with prams, approaching from both directions. Alan drove on slowly and was halted by a stout crossing-patrol warden in her flat cap and overall, with her 'lollipop' banner, outside the primary school.

He had plenty of time to observe the bright new building with its large playground as he waited while the shoal of children filed across the road. It was all very different from when his own daughter was a child and went to the village school in Lower Holtbury, where all the pupils were taught by one woman in a Victorian building with few amenities, and where Pauline had received an excellent start to a school career that had been continued at Stowburgh grammar school and then a teachers' training college. The village school in Lower Holtbury was closed now, and the children went by bus to High Holtbury.

Where had the years gone, Alan wondered, sliding the car into gear as the lollipop lady allowed him to move. One minute Pauline had been a little thing, like these mites all trooping in to school. Now she was married to a veterinary surgeon whom she'd met on a walking holiday in the Alps. They lived in York, and Pauline was expecting her first baby.

Alan drove into the town centre and found a slot in the multistorey municipal car park. He sat there for some minutes in the concrete gloom, staring at the grey wall ahead of him. The whole day stretched ahead to be filled, for Alan was out of work.

One afternoon some weeks ago, the managing director of Biggs and Cooper, a light engineering firm at Stowburgh where Alan had worked for nearly twenty-five years, had summoned him to his own office. Officially, the working day was over; the managing director's secretary had gone home and the last stragglers were departing from the building. The managing director's office, though comfortable, with charcoal carpet tiles on the floor and black leather-covered armchairs for informal chats, was by no means ostentatious. When Alan came in, the managing director was seated behind his paperless desk. He bade Alan be seated opposite him, took his half-moon spectacles off, polished them and replaced them, then took them off again, frowning. Gravely, he spoke about rising costs, lower turnover, the need to retrench and cut down. He put his spectacles back on his nose and picked up a paperknife that lay on the desk before him, inspecting it closely. Alan understood the message before it was put into words.

'But why me?' he had asked. 'My experience – the sales figures, taking into account the difficult times, are not so bad – ' His voice had tailed away as the managing director broke in to explain that the sales system was being restructured, slimmed down, jobs dovetailed one with another. Brian Clark would be undertaking work that formerly had been Alan's responsibility, combining home sales with the export area. The firm was not large enough to carry two such posts under the reorganization, he said suavely.

The managing director, who was the same age as Alan, did not like what he was doing now; but when weeding out staff, as with the garden, the weaker specimens must go so that the strong might thrive. Alan, though he was painstakingly conscientious, efficient and popular, and certainly very experienced, lacked drive; he was not ruthless, and today ruthlessness was often vital in the business jungle. Besides, he was nearly fifty, while Brian Clark was only thirty-three: a tough, aggressive young man approaching his prime, the better long-term investment.

'There will be the usual compensation of course – tide you over – after so long – ' the managing director pushed back his chair and made as if to rise, indicating the end of their talk. He felt great relief; there would be no scene. ' – excellent testimonial, of course – ' he went on. ' – wish you luck – ' The disconnected phrases fell softly on Alan's ears, meaningless platitudes.

Alan did not go straight home. He drove around for a while, then stopped, most unusually for him, at The Grapes in High Holtbury, where he had two large whiskies to help him break the news to his wife.

Daphne was out playing bridge when he reached home. Two years ago she had taken it up, attending evening classes to learn the rudiments after their daughter Pauline got married, and now, apart from some regular sessions every week, she was often in demand to make up a four if someone dropped out. That had happened this evening. She'd left a note for him, and his dinner in the oven where it had got rather dry.

When she came in, quite late, flushed and pleased, having won thirty-five pence, Alan could not bring himself to deflate her by telling her what had happened. It would keep until the next day.

But next day no suitable moment seemed to arrive, and as time passed it grew harder and harder to find the appropriate chance, for Daphne was always so busy.

She still did not know he had lost his job. Alan had left home at the usual time this morning, but instead of driving to Stowburgh he had turned off at the roundabout on the main road and driven to Berbridge, the county town.

He felt deeply humiliated. He had always worked hard and people had trusted him. If he guaranteed a delivery date, the customer knew the promise would be honoured. Young Brian Clark, with his tight, tapered trousers, his bright ties, his cropped hair brushed forward, and his tinted spectacles, was quite different: he was always on the move, was talkative and persuasive, stirring things up. In fairness, Alan had to admit that he had built up the export side of the business, and ahead of the young man lay his best twenty years, whilst Alan's were in the nature of things, in the past.

God, he was beginning to think like a grandfather! He'd better forget about that while he was job-hunting; it might sound as if he were ready for felt slippers and an armchair by the hearth.

Alan had already registered with the Professional and Executive Recruitment Bureau. There was a private agency in Berbridge, where he intended to put down his name, and he must sign on at the Department of Social Security. He would tell the agency not to telephone him at home about any prospective job and arrange, instead, to ring them daily. He had bought his white Cortina from Biggs and Cooper at an advantageous price; this was something often possible if you became redundant. He'd need the car for driving to interviews.

He made his calls in the town; then, in the public library, he searched through the likely newspapers for possible vacancies, settling at a table near a window to write applications for the few that seemed appropriate. The employment agency had given him two possibilities, though warning him that the respective firms really wanted men in their thirties. He'd had his *curriculum vitae* typed before he left Biggs and Cooper, and had a stock of photocopies of the short document, the sole contents now of his large, worn briefcase. At the shiny light oak table in the library, Alan looked at it from the viewpoint of a prospective employer. Though he understood every aspect of the management of a small, specialized works, he could not make, with his own hands, any of its products. He had no university degree, nor any sort of diploma. During his national service in the army he had learned no trade, but had made the most of his chance to see a little of the world, had some amorous adventures, and gained confidence in himself as a man. He had risen no higher than the rank of lance-corporal. Alan's papers attested to his loyalty, application and honesty: that was all. How valuable today were these once prized qualities?

His courage wavered, sitting in the library carefully writing, with his Waterman pen, what was virtually the same letter several times. His handwriting was clear and regular; that, at least, should be an asset. He'd heard that some firms obtained a graphologist's assessment before awarding a post to an otherwise suitable applicant. At least

14

the wives of aspiring sales and production managers were not yet inspected, as well as their husbands, he reflected.

All Alan's attempts to tell Daphne that he had lost his job had failed. They had few opportunities for conversation, since she seldom sat still, even for meals. In the mornings she was always hurrying off, either to Stowburgh hospital, where twice a week she worked in the occupational therapy department, or to the golf course where she played on most other days. She was rarely at home for long in the evenings as she had regular bridge and badminton appointments.

Daphne had been the games mistress at the girls' grammar school in the town where, after his national service, Alan had worked in a surveyor's office. He intended to qualify, and had not planned to marry for years; his salary was too small to support a wife, which in those days most husbands expected to do. When he met Daphne his thinking changed. He took her out in his old Morris and they walked in the country; her vitality and physical energy were what first attracted him to her, and he joined the badminton club of which she was a member so that they might meet more often, though he had no aptitude for that or any game. They held hands in cinemas, and had tea at the Tudor Café on Saturdays if there was no match at Daphne's school. They slid into an engagement, the natural result, both thought, of the increasing warmth of their kisses when he took her home.

Alan had abandoned the surveyor's office to look for a job with ultimate prospects and, currently, a higher salary. Biggs and Cooper were expanding at the time and had a vacancy for a clerk. Alan got the position and had been with the firm ever since, moving through several departments. Soon after their marriage Daphne became pregnant, which solved the problem of whether or not she should keep on her job, and perhaps their one real disappointment had been that Pauline was their only child.

Through the years Daphne kept busy, involved with village activities in Lower Holtbury and with rearing Pauline. She played tennis all the year round when the weather allowed, and badminton in the winter. Later, as

Pauline grew older, she took up golf, and it was golf that led her to bridge, for often, after a morning round, the ladies would settle down to a rubber or two in the comfortable clubhouse. For Daphne, Cherry Cottage was the base from which she set forth to engage in real life in the world outside; for Alan, it was a refuge where he could potter in peace in the garden, or in his study, where he kept his record player and most of his books.

One night Alan had tried, in bed, to get Daphne to listen to him. Normally he slept well, but lately he had lain awake, worrying about his coming redundancy, while Daphne breathed evenly beside him.

He had waited, pretending to read, while Daphne bathed and creamed her face, and when she got into bed he took off his glasses, closed his book and turned to her. Daphne slid her arms round him at once, misinterpreting. She had the same healthy, uncomplicated attitude to sex as she had to most aspects of life, and though a little surprised, for it was Wednesday and latterly they had tended to reserve such moments mainly for weekends, she was really rather pleased. It made her feel quite young again, and giggly.

Alan did not destroy her mood. Why distress her? The news would keep, and things could be a great deal worse than in fact they were, for the mortgage was paid off, Pauline was settled, and his compensation, after so long with Biggs and Cooper, would be substantial. All he had to do now was to leave Cherry Cottage at his usual time every day and return as before. She would suspect nothing, and there was small risk of her finding out what had happened by accident. She never telephoned him at the office. They had no rule about it; simply, the need had not arisen since Pauline's appendicitis when she was twelve. He had sometimes called Daphne, in the early years, but now only did so if he was unexpectedly delayed at the office, and that was rare. None of her golfing friends or hospital colleagues had any connection with Biggs and Cooper; no one from the works lived in the Holtbury area; and he and Daphne did not meet anyone from the firm socially. Their friends, he reflected, were really Daphne's friends, not his; anyone who came to dinner or drinks was either from the village or a golfing contact of Daphne's. He'd never really noticed that before. Well, it was lucky things had worked out like that, he decided now. He should be safe from discovery until he had found another job and could tell her both bits of news together.

At one o'clock in the library on that first Monday, Alan put his papers away in his briefcase. He'd have a sandwich in a pub somewhere, but how should he spend the afternoon? There was plenty to do at home – sweeping up storm damage in the garden and having a bonfire, for instance, since the weather was good – but he couldn't do these things without some sort of explanation to Daphne.

He collected the car and drove to the Rising Sun on the edge of the town, where he had a snack lunch which cost him much more than his subsidized meals in the works canteen. Then he bought stamps for his letters and mailed them. There would be younger applicants for all these positions and most would be equipped with business diplomas, if not degrees. Alan sighed. He'd spent all that time in the surveyor's office without achieving any qualification, though he knew a lot about housing, drainage and planning, which had been useful when they had an extension built on to Cherry Cottage.

It was just after two o'clock. Alan went along to the town museum, which he hadn't visited since he took Pauline years ago, and stayed there nearly an hour, but how could he occupy the rest of the afternoon?

He could go to the cinema.

What a pity the old Plaza no longer existed, he thought, settling into the Cortina and reaching under the dash for the Murraymints he kept there for long journeys or frustrations in traffic jams. He was not far from its site, and the new shopping centre near the primary school. He'd go along there and buy some more Murraymints and the local paper to see what was on at the cinema. He had a whole week to fill in, so he might as well study the available diversions. The week might extend to several: even to months.

As he passed the school once more, the children had just come out, some on foot, in groups, or walking off with their mothers. Others, fetched by car, were driven away. The lollipop lady, her job almost done, had moved to the kerb with her banner.

Alan saw the small girl quite alone. She was some fifty yards beyond the school, standing on the corner looking along the road. While he watched, she moved suddenly, seeming to square her small shoulders, and began to walk on, purposefully. She was very small. Blonde hair in two bunches stuck out below her red woollen cap. She wore white socks, above which her knees were bare.

Alan passed her slowly. She seemed very young to be on her way home alone.

He drove on, turned the corner into the street with the shops, and parked outside the supermarket. At the news-agent's, he bought a packet of Murraymints and the *Berbridge Bulletin*. Then he sat in the car reading the cinema announcements. There was only the Odeon now, with its three screens, and the titles of their offerings held no obvious allure, but one sounded as if it might be a Western; he could pass an hour or so watching shoot-outs and galloping horses, Alan decided, folding up the paper.

As he reached for the ignition key, he glanced casually ahead at the shoppers on the pavement and caught sight of the small girl he had noticed earlier. She was walking along, head held high, towards his parking spot. Just before reaching him she turned into a baker's shop. Alan waited, curious. In a few minutes the child emerged, now carrying a paper bag. She came to the kerb edge and looked carefully in each direction. Then she stepped into the road between Alan's car and the one ahead, and peered each way once more. She had a thin, pale, anxious face. Her hair, beneath the red cap, was like flax.

Where was the child's mother, wondered Alan angrily, and why was there no pedestrian crossing to serve these shops? He glanced in his side mirror. The road seemed clear. The child took a step forward, hesitating, then retreated again between the two cars, her head poking forward. Alan saw it was safe for her to cross and nodded encouragingly, but she was oblivious, intent on the road.

His hand was on the door handle, about to get out and

help her, when she seized her courage and ran across, dropping to a sedate walk again on the far pavement. Alan saw her continue down the road for perhaps seventy yards to the next intersection; here she turned right, marching onwards, satchel bobbing on her back, paper bag under one arm and white socks twinkling above little brown ankle boots.

He started the car and moved slowly out of his parking spot when the traffic allowed. Taking the centre of the road, he indicated his intention to turn and went down the road into which the child had disappeared; Oak Way, it said on the corner. He came up to her quite soon; she was too small to have got very far.

3

Tessa Waring walked quickly along Oak Way. The worst part of her journey back from school was over now, and she quite liked doing this last stretch alone. The bad bit was at the beginning, not knowing if Mummy would be standing near the tree on the corner; she always waited there, when she did come, staying close to the wall until Tessa had run up to her and was holding her hand, and even then she would walk along almost touching the hedge or fence or wall that they were passing. She hated crossing roads and going into shops and all sorts of things that happened every day, going pale and shaky, and frightening Tessa by looking so strange.

Several other small children were never met at school because their mothers had jobs which didn't finish till later. Some went off together, but there was no other child among them who lived in Oak Way. Usually, Tessa walked back through the recreation ground; then she did not need to cross any busy roads; but sometimes there was shopping she had to do if Mummy wasn't there to meet her. Today she'd had to buy a loaf. It was still warm inside its bag under her arm. The bakery had smelled lovely, and the lady behind the counter had been the nice one with the round glasses and smiley eyes, not the one with the fierce black eyebrows and stiff hair that Tessa was sure was a wig.

Mummy had a wig. It was soft and curling, and could be brushed into various styles. Mummy never wore it now but Tessa used it for dressing up, when she was being a princess or a space siren. Mummy's own hair was very straight, like Tessa's, though much darker. She said it had been just as pale as Tessa's when she was a little girl.

Each afternoon, Tessa would come out of school with a funny, excited feeling inside, looking for Mummy. Then, when she wasn't there, a sort of collapse would happen and the bright feeling would be replaced by an ache, which Tessa would try to ignore as she walked home, pretending that she'd known all along Mummy wouldn't have come and wasn't really disappointed, but sometimes there would be a tear or two to blink back. This would be specially the case if Tessa was in a hurry to tell Mummy something extra good – that she'd got a gold star, for instance – or indeed if things had gone wrong, like a problem with numbers or a bad tumble in the playground. Mostly, school was nice; Mrs Dawson, the teacher, though quite old, was a laughy sort of person and you knew what to expect of the day. Tessa didn't like surprises much; they weren't always nice.

Once, there had been a different school, a much smaller one, and other children she'd always known because they lived near each other and had all been to playgroup together first. Mummy had been different then, always able to take her to school and meet her; and there'd been Daddy, too. They'd lived in a house with a garden that belonged just to them, and she'd had a swing of her own. Now they lived in a flat that was part of a very old house, and they shared the garden with other people.

Mummy had explained that Daddy had gone away, and Granny Waring, who'd come to stay, had said he was living in heaven with Grandpa and Jesus, but it was all rather puzzling to Tessa. Vivid in her memory was that last morning: the angry voices and banging door, then Daddy driving away in his car. He'd forgotten to kiss her goodbye, which he always did even when he was cross with Mummy. For ages she'd expected him to come back just to do that, if not to stay, but they'd moved and now, if he came, he wouldn't know where they were. But people didn't come back from heaven, ever. She knew that.

At first, when they moved, Mummy had a job. She'd said that jobs fitting in with school hours would be easier to find in Berbridge when she explained about selling the house, but Tessa knew there wasn't much money now. Daddy had taken that, and the car, too, when he went to heaven.

It had been nice to begin with; she and Mummy had painted the flat and made it comfy. Tessa liked the big garden, which had lots of bushes and trees and easily became an enchanted forest. There was a plot where Mr Henshaw from the ground floor flat grew vegetables; he sometimes gave them things from it – cauliflowers and cabbages, peas and beans, when there were plenty. She and Mummy had the first floor flat, which was reached by their very own separate staircase, an iron one outside the building. Mrs Cox, in the basement, had her own private stairs too. Mummy took temporary jobs because then she could be with Tessa all the holidays. They'd visited Grandmother – that was Mummy's mother – in Cornwall, and had gone fishing in a boat several times; Tessa had liked that.

It was soon after they came back that things started to go wrong and Mummy kept feeling ill. One morning on the way to school she'd gone all white and peculiar-looking, and had clung to the fence of the house they were passing, swaying about so that Tessa had been afraid she would fall down. She'd put her arms round her, to hold her up. Mummy had stood up properly then and told Tessa to go on to school by herself; she'd go home, she said, and lie down, and would soon be all right. All day, Tessa had worried, but Mummy had been outside as usual that afternoon.

After that, though, things had got worse and Mummy had often felt strange. She'd got an attack of the gremlins, she'd say, with a funny sort of laugh that didn't sound as if it was a joke at all. She didn't go out to work now but did typing at home, and she hardly left the flat unless Tessa was with her.

This afternoon, carefully carrying her loaf, Tessa turned in at the gate of 51 Oak Way. She walked along the moss-covered path that led round the side of the tall old house to what had once been the tradesmen's entrance. Here, stairs led down to Mrs Cox's basement flat, where the door opened straight into her dark living-room with its long barred windows. Past this gloomy area, Tessa walked on to the curly iron stairs leading up to the first floor flat. At the top she set her parcel down, took off one red woollen glove, and fished inside her clothes. Round her neck, under her clothes, the doorkey hung on a tape.

She drew it out and unlocked the door, then tucked the key back against her vest before picking up her parcel and going inside. Everything that Tessa undertook was done with care, for so much depended upon her.

She closed the door and called out, in her high, clear voice, 'Mummy?'

'Here, darling.'

Louise Waring hurried to greet her daughter. She was small and thin, with large blue eyes, shadows under them, and a pale face. She hugged Tessa, taking the parcel containing the loaf, and began helping her off with her coat. It had been a bad day today, and she had been sitting in her chair huddled by the gas fire, trembling, her gaze on the clock, waiting for Tessa's return; then, when the child did arrive, she was unable to move to the door. She'd tried, earlier, to go to meet her, as she tried every day, but had got no further than the laurel bush by the side of the house before one of the shaking attacks, which made her heart pound and her head spin and which she called 'the gremlins', began, and she had to return to the sanctuary of the flat.

It would be better tomorrow. She told herself that every day, and one day it had to be true. Now, with Tessa there, she was able to smile.

'Let's have dripping toast for tea, shall we?' she said.

She wanted to tell Tessa how she tried to set out every day to meet her and not let the child think her neglectful or uncaring, but it was impossible to explain something she did not understand herself.

'It's shock,' the doctor had said, prescribing tranquillizers. 'Very natural, under the circumstances. It will wear off, given time.'

But it was taking so long.

Louise felt so dull and stupid these days. Sometimes she feared she was losing her mind, and if that were to happen what would become of Tessa? She must pull herself together. Other women showed much more courage than she was doing, and in far worse circumstances, too. No wonder, before they moved, her few friends had faded away. She'd always been nervous and shy and she'd had such a shock when she found out how much money Roddy owed that she'd wanted to hide away from people they knew. She'd had to sell the house to pay Roddy's creditors and a new start seemed the best way to forget.

'Tell me what happened at school,' she said to Tessa. 'Did you have singing?'

Gradually, in the warmth of the small kitchen, with the light on and the blinds drawn, the tension left both of them. Tessa was an ordinary little girl again in a protected atmosphere, chattering away, showing her mother her drawing and writing. Louise, enclosed too, was no longer alone and knew that she need make no further effort until the next day when again she would try to take Tessa to school. She listened, looked and admired. After tea they played Snap, and then, curled up on the sofa together, read a further instalment of *The Borrowers*.

Louise, full of pills, slept heavily that night, with her bedroom door ajar so that if Tessa called out she would wake, and a low bulb burning on the landing.

Down below, in the basement flat, Mrs Cox slept, too. She seldom dreamed of the past now, but a blue light always burned in her bedroom throughout the night, just in case.

The houses in Oak Way had been built during the expansion of Berbridge between the wars. Some were arranged in semidetached pairs; others, like number 51, were large and detached, and several of these had been converted into flats.

Louise knew none of the other tenants well. They all, except Mrs Cox in the basement, went out to work each weekday. There were two girls with office jobs in the two flatlets, really bed-sitters, on the top floor. The young couple on the ground floor, the Henshaws, had the biggest part of the house. Terence, at weekends and on summer evenings, was often to be seen working in the garden, and he and his wife seemed friendly; they had asked Louise down for a drink once or twice but she had always refused; she would not leave Tessa alone.

Mrs Cox was short and sturdy. Out of doors, she always wore a severe felt hat over her cropped grey hair. Sometimes she strolled in the garden, though she never sat out in the sun as the other tenants did. Last year, when a poisoned finger prevented Terence Henshaw from clipping the boundary hedge, she did it for him, even burning the clippings afterwards. Though a pensioner, she was fit and active. Tessa, playing at being a princess in a forest or an explorer in the jungle, would pretend, if they met, that Mrs Cox was a witch. Mrs Cox always drew attention to an untied shoelace or a descending sock, which was irritating, but sometimes she invited Tessa into her flat and there would be a glass of milk and a round small cake full of sultanas for her, or a banana, which Mrs Cox would cut into very thin slices and expect her to eat with a spoon, which seemed a bit complicated.

Mrs Cox's sitting-room was quite big, but it was gloomy because the barred windows looked into the well and let in very little light, though you could see the legs of anyone passing on the path outside. Mrs Cox was fussy, and would spread a little cloth on the table before you had your milk and cake. There were white cloths on the backs of the chairs, too. There were only two armchairs; a tall one and a much rounder one which Tessa preferred. Tessa had told Mummy about the white cloths on their backs and she said they were called antimacassars and had been necessary long ago when men put oil on their hair to smarm it down and the oil rubbed off on the chairs.

But there was no Mr Cox now. Tessa hadn't liked to ask where he was; she didn't like it when people asked about Daddy.

There were a lot of photographs in Mrs Cox's sitting-room, all of children. Many were babies in prams – funny-looking prams, very big and deep and with large hoods. Mrs Cox could be seen in some of the photographs, always dressed in a hat rather like the one she wore now, and a long plain coat.

'Are they all your children, Mrs Cox?' Tessa had asked her once, and Mrs Cox had said yes. She certainly had a very big family, Tessa thought.

On days when Tessa came home from school through the recreation ground, Mrs Cox was sometimes there, on a seat near the swings, or strolling back from the path by the river which flowed past beyond the railings. They would walk together then, which Tessa found trying because she liked to run part of the way as she always wanted to get back to Mummy quickly. Once, though, it had been lucky, for there had been a big dog which had come bounding towards her, only wanting to play, Tessa was sure, but it was just like a wolf and she had been frightened. Mrs Cox had driven it off with her umbrella, and when its owner came up had scolded him for letting the dog run wild. The man had got cross and said some rude things to Mrs Cox, but he'd put the dog on a lead and taken it away.

There were so many hazards, coming back from school on her own. She mustn't speak to strangers, especially men in cars who would offer her sweets. Men in cars sometimes stole children away and were cruel to them, Mummy had said. There was the traffic, which came along so fast just when you thought the road was clear. There were big boys on bikes, who swooped past you and sometimes specially went through puddles to splash you, or rode right at you, only turning away at the very last minute. There was the dragon that lived behind the holly bush on the corner of Oak Way, and if you didn't hurry past his fiery breath would devour you.

It was such a relief to survive all these perils and reach home safely, where nothing could hurt you. And Mummy must surely soon be better: all those pills would do some good in the end.

Tessa hadn't noticed the white Cortina that followed her slowly home.

4

Daphne Parker was home by five o'clock that evening. She had spent a busy and rewarding day at the hospital, where the boy with the calliper was getting stronger daily, and old Mrs Burt, who had had a stroke, was talking intelligibly and would soon be able to leave; she could no longer live on her own and her son had adapted, under Daphne's guidance, a room in his house for his mother.

She thought about these agreeable events as she chopped vegetables to add to the curry sauce in which she intended to immerse the remains of the half shoulder of lamb she and Alan had had for lunch the day before. She heard his key in the door just as she had subconsciously started to listen for it. He came into the kitchen, kissed her on the cheek and then filled the kettle and switched it on. This was unusual and she looked at him in surprise.

'I thought a cup of tea would be nice,' Alan explained. In fact he was missing the extra large mugful his secretary, Stephanie, had always brought him in the afternoon at the office, and sucking sweets had increased the thirst that was habit.

He did look tired, Daphne thought.

'Why not a sherry?' she suggested.

'No thanks, dear. Tea will be just the thing,' Alan said. 'How was your day?'

While the kettle boiled she told him, in detail, and he expressed pleasure in hearing about Mrs Burt's progress with the walking frame.

'And you?' Daphne asked, in her turn.

She thought that one of the nicest things about marriage

was talking over the separate day at the end of it; it kept you in touch with each other. When Pauline was young and she had been tied, Alan had never been too preoccupied about business or too weary to listen to what Daphne planned to do about Pauline's music lessons (allow her to give them up) or her wish for a new tennis racket. Daphne's aims for their only child had always seemed reasonable enough to Alan, and he'd left decisions to her. Life had flowed harmoniously on through the years with only minor disagreements about what colour to paint the bathroom and where to go for the annual holiday.

Alan had made the tea.

'Will you have a cup?' he asked her.

'No thanks.' Daphne shook her head. Tea was an integral part of her hospital day. 'Everything all right at the office?' she said, to prompt him.

What if he told her the truth? Described his day in Berbridge with the hours at the library? Even mentioned the small girl too young to walk home from school alone, whom he'd followed? Told her about the film he'd watched part of – he'd missed the beginning – in the end not the Western but a sensitive effort in French, with subtitles, about adolescents in the Ardennes? It hadn't been the sex tangle he'd expected from the posters outside the cinema but a poignant tale of misunderstanding amid beautiful scenery. What if he said, 'I'm out of a job and on the dole, and if I don't find something before my redundancy pay is spent, we'll have to sell up and change our whole way of life'?

'Oh, much as usual,' he said, pouring his tea. It came to him now that he could invent small items of news that would be safe to offer Daphne, for she would have no means of checking them. 'Stephanie's thinking of leaving,' he added. In a sense it was true: Stephanie, his secretary for the past three years, was now working for the managing director.

'Oh Alan! That's bad! Why?' exclaimed Daphne. 'Or is she pregnant at last?'

'No,' Alan said. He had followed Stephanie's periodic moods and had shared her hopes and disappointments through most of their time together. 'I think she feels a change of scene might help,' he said.

'It's probably Vincent,' Daphne pronounced. 'He's rather difficult, isn't he? Do talk her out of it.' She knew that Alan thought highly of Stephanie, despite her somewhat mercurial temperament.

They discussed the possible stresses in the home life of Stephanie and her husband Vincent until their meal was ready, and afterwards Daphne went off to play badminton.

Alan went into his study and put on his new recording of *Trovatore*. While he listened to it, he did some sketches, in pencil, of the small girl he had seen that day. He drew well. He could have lessons now, he thought idly, lightly shading the hollows behind her thin little knees in a sketch of her walking away from the viewer. There would be plenty of time for study.

A week passed, and Alan was settling to his new routine.

Every morning he went to Berbridge Central Library to search through the newspaper advertisements and write applications for possible jobs. Then, on his way to post them, he called at the employment agency. In that first week he made one personal approach to a firm on their books. He saw the personnel manager who said he would be considered for the vacant post, but they were in fact looking for someone considerably younger.

At lunchtime he went to various pubs or snack bars for a sandwich, and in the afternoon he returned to the library where he settled down comfortably to read. He should, he supposed, follow some purposeful course of instruction, but he was rather enjoying dipping about in books that caught his fancy. He had read Sir Arthur Grimble's *A Pattern of Islands* which he came on by chance, and had now embarked on a life of Verdi, which he replaced each day on the shelf.

At Biggs and Cooper's works he had had his own reserved parking slot in the yard, which of course was free. Now, using the municipal multistorey car park every day, he was spending a large sum daily just on leaving the car. He was using more petrol, too, than before. His daily budget, with no salary coming in, had gone up, and this couldn't continue.

On the second Monday morning, he drove straight through Berbridge as he had done the week before. So consistent was his timing that again he met the blue Fiesta waiting at the side road near the traffic lights, and again he waved it on.

This time, Alan did not follow the Fiesta as far as the school. He turned into Oak Way, along which he had followed the small girl the previous week, where there was plenty of space to park without charge by the kerb. Then he walked back to the main road and caught a bus in to the town centre.

On Tuesday morning he saw the small girl again. This time, he left the car in Shippham Avenue, a cul-de-sac that led off Oak Way and ended in the entrance to the recreation ground.

As he parked in the short road, Alan saw the little girl running along ahead of him, and he glanced at his watch. She was going to be late for school, he thought, though she wasn't taking the route past the shops, as before.

Vague fears that she might cross the road recklessly in her haste came into his mind. Children moved so quickly and were so easily distracted. He got out of the car, locked it, and followed her into the recreation ground. She was still running.

In procession they crossed the short, damp turf, past the swings and the see-saw, and through the gate at the end where the child slowed down. Alan, his long strides closing the gap between them, saw the pale stem of her neck above the coat collar, the two bunches of ash-blonde hair emerging beneath her woolly cap. He noticed again the shadowed hollows behind her bare knees above the white socks. She hurried on.

Beyond the recreation ground, Alan saw the school, with no further road to cross. The lollipop lady had gone, and there were no other children in sight as the little girl reached the school entrance and ran in. Were you punished for being late at that age? he wondered. Perhaps she bore some letter of explanation.

He pondered about the child during the day. Modern children were extremely self-reliant, he knew, and were taught by their enlightened parents how to cross the road almost as soon as they could walk. Yet there had been a desperate urgency about the little girl this morning. Wondering about her and her possible problems took his mind off his own.

That afternoon he walked back from the town centre in time to station himself, on foot, outside the school but at a little distance, before the children came out. He watched for the little girl.

He saw the blue Fiesta. The young woman driver got out and walked up to the gates to collect five children. They hung round her, two with mops of dark curls like her own, the others fairer.

The little blonde girl was one of the last children to come through the school gates. Alan saw her look across towards the corner opposite where he was standing. Then, as before, she seemed to square her shoulders before going over the road herself, under the benediction of the lollipop lady's banner.

She set off resolutely, bound for the shops again, Alan guessed as he slowly followed. Her thin little white-socked legs twinkled ahead. This time, she went into the supermarket, picking up a wire basket at the doorway and walking a short way into the shop to where there was a small space by the biscuits. Here she set her basket down on the ground, then pulled her satchel round to the front of her body, unbuckled it, and hunted inside. She took out a piece of paper and consulted it. Alan could see her mouthing the words; she was barely old enough to read.

She put her shopping list, for so it must be, away, picked up the wire basket and headed towards the freezer area. Alan had picked up a basket too. He put a packet of cheese crackers in it; he ought to buy snacks for his lunch instead of spending money in pubs. He moved towards the small girl.

She was standing on her toes, stretching, trying to reach something deep inside the freezer cabinet.

'Can I help you?' Alan smiled down at her. Her hand, in

30

its red glove, was hovering above the fish fingers. He picked up a packet and gave it to her. 'Is this what you want?'

'Yes, thank you,' she said gravely, putting it in her basket with a packet of peas which she had been able to reach herself. She did not look at him, but moved on round the shop to take a tin of rice pudding from another shelf, and a pot of cherry jam. She collected the items with slow deliberation, reading the labels with concentration.

Alan, with two packets of Murraymints alongside the cheese crackers in his own basket, went to a different till at the check-out. He saw the assistant who was dealing with the small girl smile at her, and help her pack her purchases into a plastic carrier which the child had pulled from her satchel. The little girl looked quite animated as they exchanged some remarks. Then solemnity returned as she left the shop and crossed the wide pavement to wait at the kerb before crossing the road.

Alan stood beside her, planning to write to the *Berbridge Bulletin* about the need for a pedestrian crossing here. He looked to right and left, as the child did, and crossed beside her. Her bundle of shopping, in relation to her own size, was large and heavy. She had no doubt been told not to talk to strangers, and would not take it well if he offered to carry it home for her. He walked behind her, however, all the way to number 51 Oak Way, and saw her go safely inside.

After that he looked for her every morning, parking his car in such a way that if he was sitting in it, he would see her approaching the recreation ground. In the afternoons, if she went shopping, he waited outside the row of shops until she emerged with whatever she had to buy that day, not speaking to her, merely making sure that she crossed safely over the road and reached home without mishap. Some afternoons, if it was fine, he walked through the recreation ground and along the towpath beside the river. He would stroll past cabin cruisers moored at the bank, their canopies tightly fastened now against the winter. He still missed his afternoon cup of tea and would sometimes call at a café for one before going back to where he had parked.

He would return to the car before it grew dark, and sit there reading or listening to the radio, occasionally running the engine to let the heater come into action when he felt cold. He did not go to the cinema again.

On Wednesday of the second week, the handle of the little girl's carrier bag broke as she crossed the main road, and three oranges rolled away from her. Other packages – biscuits and a bag of flour – fell too.

Alan was beside her in an instant.

'Run across – quick – it's all right, I'll pick it all up,' he said. 'Quick, now – go along, before a car comes.'

But tears were near. She looked at Alan with brimming, glistening eyes, and did not move.

Alan took her hand.

'Don't cry,' he said, holding onto her while a car went past swerving slightly to avoid an orange, the driver hooting in annoyance and frowning at Alan for, as he supposed, causing the confusion. 'It's all right,' he repeated, and led her over the road to the further pavement. 'You wait there. Give me your bag and I'll rescue your shopping.'

He took the carrier from her, waited for a space in the oncoming traffic, and returned to the road where he retrieved the packages. Luckily there was only a small tear in the bag of flour and it had escaped being crushed by a passing car. A woman had picked up one of the errant oranges and she gave Alan a curious inspection as she dropped it into the bag he extended towards her.

'She lives just down Oak Way,' Alan told the woman. 'I'll see her home.'

The woman nodded. She had noticed the child alone before but the man seemed to know her, and in his tweed overcoat, with his greying hair neatly brushed, he looked utterly respectable.

The little girl was waiting anxiously on the far pavement, a few tears rolling down her face. Alan gave her a clean handkerchief.

'Here – blow your nose,' he said. 'It's all right now. I'll carry your bundle home for you.'

Obediently, she blew and wiped, and when she had returned his handkerchief, he rummaged in his pocket for a Murraymint which, after a moment's hesitation, she accepted. She knew this kind man. She'd seen him outside school when she was looking for Mummy, and in a white car near the rec. He'd helped her once, too, when she couldn't reach something in the supermarket. So he wasn't really a stranger.

Sucking her Murraymint, Tessa Waring walked along beside Alan and told him her name and that she was nearly seven years old.

They parted at the gates of 51 Oak Way, where Alan handed back her bundle, and she carried it safely inside.

Their friendship began that day.

5

These winter mornings Mrs Cox rose late, her one concession to her age.

She always woke early: habit died hard. First there had been those decades with the babies; then the other years she tried not to remember, years filled with the clanging of doors, the harsh sounds of footsteps on stone, and the smells: so many long years spent like that.

She had not always lived alone in the basement flat at 51 Oak Way. When she arrived, Mavis had been there, waiting for her, the new life already begun. But Mavis, although eight years younger, had died, leaving Mrs Cox all she possessed – some money, and the flat's furniture. Mrs Cox was just able to manage the rent on her own. For a while when she came out of prison she had done a cleaning job several days a week, but when Mavis was ill she gave that up. Now she went baby-sitting for several families living nearby, and had her regular clientele. Occasionally, if the parents planned to be very late home, she slept overnight, and it was quite like old times to stand, in dressing gown and slippers, in the small bedroom looking down at the cot with its rosy occupant dead to the world before retiring to the comfortable guest room bed herself.

Dead to the world: best not to think of that.

Waking early in her dim-lit room, Mrs Cox would get up, go to the kitchen to switch on the kettle, and visit the bathroom. Then she would put her teeth in and return to bed with a cup of tea. She would drowse for a while, remembering some of the children – Jack, in his sailor suit, perhaps, or Philip who had gone into the Foreign Office and as far as she knew was still there. She would think about Denis, who was killed in the war, and Paul, who'd become a parson.

Sometimes, she thought about Grace. Often, she slept again.

Later, she'd put on the radio and listen to the news. It always seemed gloomy, yet look what time-saving gadgets there were these days: drudgery was a thing of the past; and though people spoke of poverty, there was little to be seen in Berbridge. Young folk didn't know when they were well off.

That girl on the first floor, the mother of Tessa, now: what a spineless creature she was, to be sure, Mrs Cox thought. She didn't deserve to have such a nice, neat little girl, the feckless way she cared for her. Imagine letting a child her age walk to and from school alone, for instance; goodness knows what could happen to her. Tessa was well-behaved and polite; she played contentedly on her own by the hour, Mrs Cox knew, for she often saw her at her imaginary games in the garden. The mother was hysterical, though; Mrs Cox had come upon her one day cowering in the road, standing pressed against the fence some distance from number 51 and looking as pale as a ghost. She'd said she felt ill, and begged Mrs Cox to take her home, which Mrs Cox did.

She'd gone up with Mrs Waring into the first floor flat and lit the gas for her, and made her a cup of tea, sniffing with disapproval at what seemed to her to be simply feebleness.

'I'm sorry – I don't know why this happens – it's just since my husband – ' Mrs Waring's voice, which to Mrs Cox's ears was a self-pitying whine, had trailed off.

'Left you, has he?' Mrs Cox had said, putting sugar in

the mug – she could find no cups and saucers – and stirring vigorously.

'Well – it was – ' Louise had begun, but Mrs Cox had cut in.

'You must think of the child, my dear. Take a grip on yourself. Plenty of women bring up children alone, and nowadays no one need starve.'

It might have been Louise's own mother speaking.

'I know. I'm lucky,' Louise had said. Mrs Cox had got it all wrong but she felt too weak to explain that Roddy was dead. 'It's just that I get these funny swimmy turns,' she said.

'And I expect you've been to the doctor and he's given you pills,' said Mrs Cox.

'That's right. He said it would pass, in time,' said Louise. 'Shock, he said it was.'

'You must pull yourself together,' Mrs Cox repeated. 'Think of the child,' and when she saw that some colour had returned to Louise's face, she left her. It was no good being soft with someone like that: it would just encourage her in her self-pitying ways.

Lately, she'd seen Tessa talking to a man – a big fellow, well dressed, and middle-aged, with greying hair. Was it the father, visiting? Mrs Cox did not know, but she meant to find out.

It was another thing to think about, lying in bed on these dark winter mornings with the electric blanket which Mavis had given her turned on, and her cup of tea at hand.

She never looked at the newspaper cuttings then. Those were for the night hours, rare now, when the dreams came and she couldn't sleep, haunted by images of little Grace.

She'd been blonde, too: just like a little angel; and she'd had a Mummy who didn't deserve such a jewel.

Sometimes, by mistake, Mrs Cox would call Tessa by her name. 'Grace,' she'd say, and Tessa would stare. But Tessa was older than Grace had been when it happened.

She asked Tessa about the grey-haired man, intercepting her one afternoon in the recreation ground on the way home from school.

'Is he your Daddy?' she asked, and the child had looked puzzled.

'No,' she said. 'He isn't at all like Daddy,' and then she had added, 'Daddy's in heaven with Jesus and Grandpa.'

So that's what her mother had told her! How wicked!

Tessa had run past Mrs Cox, waving, after this exchange, and the old woman now saw a male figure coming to meet her: the very man they'd just been discussing. They met and caught hands and with Tessa swinging on his arm, went on ahead of Mrs Cox, who stumped over the grass, muttering. Fresh growth was beginning to show; birds were twittering in the bushes, and soon the razzmatazz of spring would be here, a time Mrs Cox did not enjoy. She walked on at a steady pace, sturdy and upright, wearing thick wool stockings and zipped boots rather like Tessa's. On her head was her grey felt hat, skewered into place with a large pin thrust into the straight grey hair.

Mrs Cox turned into Oak Way. Just wait till she told Mrs Waring about the man Tessa kept meeting; she'd have something to make her tremble then, for certain. Mrs Cox looked forward to being the bearer of worrying tidings and she was thwarted indeed when she saw the man turn into the entrance of 51 with Tessa. By the time Mrs Cox came round the side of the house to her stairs, the two had vanished.

Alan had only just met Louise. The previous afternoon she had been waiting on the corner by the school when the children came out, and he had witnessed her meeting with Tessa. The little girl had halted for an instant when she saw her mother, and her delight was evident when she cast herself forward and flung her arms round the young woman who bent stiffly to greet her.

They set off together, hand in hand, the child on the outside of the pavement, the mother keeping close to the fences and walls as they passed. Tessa skipped along, chattering, a very different little girl from the quiet, intent small person he had watched on other afternoons.

He followed them, because his car was parked in Shippham Avenue, and although it was still too early to go home, he must eventually return to it although there was no need, now, to supervise Tessa's journey home.

At the shops, the pair paused outside the supermarket. They conferred briefly, and then entered together. Alan stood on the pavement, tempted to go into The Pancake for a cup of tea. Whilst he tried to make up his mind, the mother came suddenly out of the shop, moved away from its doors, and leaned against the nearby wall, taking gulps of air. Her face was ashen.

Alan went to her at once.

'Here – hold on to me,' he said. He thought she was going to faint. 'Lean forward – put your head down. I won't let you fall.'

He grasped her firmly, and Louise did as he said, bending down, clinging to his arm.

In a minute or two she felt better and straightened up. Sweat beaded her face.

'Thank you – I'll be all right now,' she said, clearly far from all right in fact.

'Take it gently,' Alan instructed. 'Breathe deeply.'

'It's stupid – I felt dizzy,' the girl said. 'I get like this sometimes.'

Perhaps she was pregnant, Alan thought. That might explain why she could not escort her daughter to and from school.

'You'll be all right in a minute,' he said.

A little colour had returned to her face. Suddenly aware of the way she was clutching his sleeve, she released him, but Alan still held her arm.

'What about Tessa?' he asked. 'Is she doing your shopping?'

Louise still felt too fragile to take in the fact that this helpful stranger knew her daughter's name.

'Yes. She'll manage,' she said. 'I'll wait here till she comes out. Please don't bother about me.'

'My car's not far away. I'll fetch it and drive you both home,' Alan said.

'Oh no – really – ' the girl protested.

'We'll just wait for Tessa,' said Alan. 'Don't try to talk. Just keep breathing deeply.'

A few passers-by glanced at them curiously, but whatever was wrong seemed to be under control. Soon Tessa came out of the supermarket, with a laden carrier which Alan at once took from her.

'Tessa, you wait here with your mother. She seems all right now but I'm going to get the car and drive you home,' he said.

Tessa had been worrying all the way round the shop, wondering how she was going to get both her mother and the shopping back to the flat.

'Oh, yes please,' she gasped with relief.

'You know that man,' Louise said, when Alan had gone. She was feeling much better now though her knees were still weak. She had felt so pleased at getting all the way to the school, earlier; on the way she had felt one of her attacks coming on, but by then was nearer to the school than home, so she had continued on her way when, after standing still for some minutes, the attack had begun to recede.

'Yes. I told you, Mummy. He's the kind man who picked up the shopping when the bag broke the other day,' Tessa said.

'Oh,' said Louise. 'I remember.'

Alan soon returned with the car, and bundled them both into it. He felt under the dash for the bag of Murraymints and handed it to Louise.

'Have one, both of you,' he said. Sugar for shock, he thought, and took one himself before putting the bag back.

When they reached 51 Oak Way, he noticed that the mother almost fled up the path, leaving him and Tessa to follow with the shopping. They caught up with her at the top of the iron staircase, where she was fumbling in her bag for the key, trembling again.

Once inside the small hallway, she turned to take the shopping from Alan.

'Thank you – ' she began, but Alan stepped over the threshold.

'I'll just take this in for you,' he said. 'And you need a cup of tea. Tessa will show me where everything is.'

'Oh but – ' Louise began.

'I could do with a cup myself,' Alan said, with a smile.

Louise owed him that. She gave in and discovered that it was nice, when you felt ill, to be taken charge of and told what to do. She went into the sitting-room and lit the gas fire, then sat down to wait while sounds of conversation came from the kitchen.

Alan and Tessa soon returned with a tray of tea, and a plate of biscuits which Tessa had arranged in an artistic design.

'My name's Alan Parker,' he told Louise, pouring out the tea. 'I've been made redundant and I'm looking for a new job, so I come to Berbridge every day to see agencies and look at the advertisements in the library. I park near here, and either take the bus or walk into the centre. I've noticed Tessa once or twice, and was luckily there when her shopping bag broke last week.'

As he explained, Alan felt a great sensation of relief. Apart from the clerks at the agency and the Social Security officials, this was the first person to whom he had revealed his circumstances.

'Oh,' said Louise. 'I'm sorry. About your job, I mean.'

'Yes – well, it was a shock, after so long,' Alan said. 'I'd been with the same firm almost all my working life, you see.'

'You'll soon find something else, won't you?'

'I hope so, but I'm a bit old, it seems, for the job market,' said Alan.

'Are you?'

Her genuine surprise was balm to Alan's hurt pride.

'Yes,' he said. 'All my experience counts for nothing.'

Louise asked what he had done, and he told her briefly, then poured her more tea. She looked much better now and was regarding him with some interest, colour in her cheeks.

'What about you?' he said at last. 'Have you seen the doctor about these turns?'

Louise nodded.

'He's given me some pills. He says they'll pass,' she said. She glanced at Tessa, who was sitting on a small stool with a glass of milk beside her, eating a large sandwich constructed by Alan with raspberry jam imprisoned between two slices of the crusty loaf she had bought the day before. 'Would you like to watch "Jackanory", Tessa?' she asked, and Tessa nodded and hopped down, crossing the room to switch on the small black-and-white television set in the corner. She moved her stool over to sit in front of it.

Alan had already glanced curiously round. He saw knitting, a sewing machine on a table, a typewriter and a neat pile of typed pages.

'Are you on your own – you and Tessa?' he asked now, certain that they were, although there was no good reason why any husband should leave signs of his presence in a sitting-room. A stranger entering the sitting-room at Cherry Cottage would have no direct evidence that a man used it, he thought; all his personal things were in his study. But there was no study here; he'd seen the extent of the flat while preparing the tea – the kitchen, two bedrooms and a bathroom, besides this room where they sat now.

'My husband was killed in a car crash last year,' Louise said flatly.

'Oh, I'm sorry. How dreadful,' said Alan. Somehow he'd expected to hear she was divorced; so many people were these days. Well, that explained things. She hadn't got over it yet.

'Roddy left a lot of debts,' Louise said, and in her turn she felt the relief of telling a stranger her troubles. 'He'd set up a mail-order business,' she went on. 'But he didn't pay his suppliers for the stock he advertised, and after a bit they wouldn't let him have any more, so he couldn't deliver, and then there were all the customers who'd sent orders and money and got no goods. He kept changing his business address, too, so that no one caught up with him. I only discovered all this afterwards. The house and everything had to be sold, to pay the creditors.' She picked at a worn place on the sofa where she was sitting. 'You never think these things will happen to you,' she said. 'There was nothing left – no insurance. He'd let the payments lapse. By the time it was all settled there was just a tiny bit over which we've got for a rainy day. We bought our furniture in junk shops.'

'What about your family?' Alan asked. 'Your parents?'

There was a silence. At last Louise said, 'My mother and I don't get on very well. She's a very successful woman. She runs a hotel in Cornwall with a partner, another woman.'

'And your father?'

Again Louise paused before she replied. When she did speak, the words burst from her.

'I thought he was dead,' she said. 'When I asked, long ago, that was what my mother told me. But then I found out that he isn't – well, he may be by now, but he didn't die when I was a child. He left my mother – ran off with someone who worked in the same place.'

'How did you discover that?' Alan asked.

'We went to stay with my mother and Ruth – that's her partner – in October,' Louise said. 'Ruth told me while we were there.'

They'd been in the bar one evening. Ruth had poured Louise a large gin and tonic and told her to relax.

'You're having a holiday,' she had said. 'Relax and enjoy yourself. Put the past behind you, Louise. You made a mistake with Roddy,' she'd continued. 'He was a selfish, insensitive man. You weren't happy with him, I know, but you would do it. You wouldn't listen to your mother, who happened to be right over that, though I don't think she always is, by any means. You need someone, Louise. I hope you'll marry again, one day.'

Louise had replied that she would be much too scared to risk a second attempt.

'That was always your trouble,' Ruth had said. 'You were always too timid.'

'But why am I like that?' Louise had demanded. 'You can't say that mother protected me too much – that's supposed to make you timid, isn't it? She doesn't know what it means to protect someone.'

'Your mother's not easy to understand,' Ruth admitted. 'But she isn't as tough as she seems. She runs away from unpleasantness – won't face it. Even with the business, I cope with the difficult interviews. Her personal life's always been a total disaster.'

Louise had stared.

'But her marriage – my father – she was shattered when he died,' she said. 'Wasn't she?'

Ruth had hesitated, then plunged.

'She was shattered all right,' she said. 'But your father didn't die, Louise. He left her. He's probably still alive.'

The news had astounded Louise.

'I don't know where he is,' she told Alan now. 'It seems Ruth only discovered he wasn't dead when the new divorce laws came in and my mother had a letter from some lawyer. She'd always refused to divorce him.'

Louise, trying to absorb what Ruth had told her, had thought this petty, but Ruth had pointed out that there were practical considerations, such as her pension, to be borne in mind.

'Did you talk to your mother about it?' Alan asked.

'Yes.' Louise had gone to the private flat, where her mother and Ruth had their rooms, after dinner that evening. Her mother always went up there when her work in the kitchen was done, while Ruth looked after the bar. The sitting-room was in semi-darkness and her mother was watching a snooker match on television. She had looked up and frowned when she saw Louise. She never looks pleased to see me, Louise had thought; I'm a big disappointment to her. 'I asked her where he lives,' she told Alan. 'She wouldn't tell me. She said I must put him out of my mind.'

Freda Hampton had been very angry.

'Ruth had no right to tell you,' she'd said. 'It's none of her business.' She'd gone on to tell Louise that she must rely only on herself, and then she would never be let down. 'Now, if that's all, I want to watch this programme,' her mother had said, turning back to the television.

Louise had wanted to know much more. She had wanted to ask what her father was like and if she resembled him. But she could ask no more of the stern woman sitting in the beige-upholstered chair.

'I started to get these funny turns after that,' Louise said to Alan. 'When we came home. My gremlins, I call them.'

'So you found out nothing more?' Alan asked.

'I did – a bit,' said Louise. She got up and went to the sideboard where, from a drawer, she took a large envelope and opened it. Inside, there was a faded photograph which she handed to Alan. It showed a wedding group, with the smiling bride in a light-coloured suit and a pillbox hat, holding a bouquet of roses. She clung to the arm of a man in air force uniform, two narrow stripes on his sleeve.

'I don't remember him at all,' Louise said.

'But you use air force slang,' Alan said gently. 'That word, gremlin, is an air force term.'

'Is it? I didn't know.'

'Where did you find the photograph?' Alan asked. 'Did your mother relent and give it to you?'

Louise shook her head.

'I stole it,' she said, and now, sitting here with this sympathetic stranger, she could laugh at what she had done. Alan thought how pretty she was when she smiled. She couldn't be much older than Pauline.

'Tell me,' he said.

'I did it our last night there,' Louise said. 'I went along to the private flat before dinner, while my mother was busy in the kitchen and Ruth was in the bar, and raided the desk.'

The sitting-room was so austere: there were three arm-chairs, a plain bookcase containing the works of Dickens and some volumes on garden management, the television set and a modern desk. Louise had never seen her mother reading for pleasure though Ruth did the crossword in the *Daily Telegraph* in lulls during the day, sitting in a sagging chair in the office, and sometimes glanced at a thriller left by a guest. Louise had opened the desk. There were a few envelopes and some of the hotel headed paper in the pigeon-holes, and a pen and some pencils; that was all. The drawers contained string, scissors, mending equipment, a box of chocolates – a surprising touch of frivolity, that, Louise had thought, amid the practicality. There was none of the usual clutter of living – no old letters, no photograph album. In the bottom drawer, under a pile of *Ideal Home* magazines, was a single photograph: the wedding group. Louise had found it hard to recognize her mother in the smiling girl on her husband's arm. She took it to her room and put it straight in her suitcase.

'I don't suppose your mother will ever discover it's gone,' Alan said.

'I don't care if she does,' Louise said. She was filled with bitter resentment against her mother who had always refused, it seemed in recollection, to let her do the things she had most desired – have flute lessons, for instance, which of course would have cost money and perhaps there wasn't enough – and who had insisted on a secretarial training when Louise had wanted to go to university. There again, expense might have been a factor, Louise had to admit, and her training had been a good and intensive one, at a private college. She had worked in the hotel, in various capacities, until she married.

'You've had a terrible time,' said Alan.

'Oh well – things were all right at first, when we came here,' Louise said. 'I had no trouble getting temporary jobs and could be with Tessa in the holidays. But when I started to get these attacks, I had to stop going out, so now I type at home.'

'It's shock,' Alan said. 'You'll get over it.'

'Well, I hope you're right, but I seem to be getting worse, not better,' said Louise. She glanced at Tessa, still sitting absorbed in front of the television. 'We had an awful row,' she said. 'Roddy and I. The morning he died, I mean. We kept having rows. He drove off in a terrible temper and overtook a lorry on a blind corner about six miles from where we lived. He hit another lorry coming towards him.' She paused. 'He took a week to die,' she added. 'It was dreadful.' Almost the worst part of it had been that she hadn't really wanted him to recover; she'd felt only horror, watching him, wires and tubes sprouting from every part of him, in the intensive care ward of the hospital. His mother had come from Majorca, and flown away again as soon as she could, which was immediately after the funeral. She'd brushed aside the question of Roddy's business disaster.

'And you've been thinking that if you hadn't quarrelled, the accident wouldn't have happened?' said Alan.

Louise nodded.

It was hardly surprising that she was in a bad state, Alan thought.

'What about friends?' he asked. She was a nice girl. She must have friends.

'Oh, people were very kind at first,' she said. 'They looked after Tessa – I had to be at the hospital, you see – and all that. But then, when I found out about the money, I felt so ashamed. I didn't want people to know.' She'd frozen them off, she realized now, those other young women, mothers of Tessa's friends; and when everything had been settled, she couldn't wait to escape. She tried to tell Alan this, and he seemed to understand.

He didn't leave until it was time for him to go home, and he said he would come again.

Mrs Cox, in her basement flat, saw his legs go past her barred windows: dark-trousered legs and feet in well-polished shoes; the legs of a man.

6

When Alan had gone, and Tessa was in bed, Louise looked again at the photograph of her father and mother. Telling Alan about her discovery had brought the shock of it back to her, and she felt restless. She paced about the flat, thinking of the time she and Tessa had spent in Cornwall. Tessa had been excited at the prospect of a seaside holiday, and Louise had set out with high hopes. People went to visit their families and were made welcome; it was part of life.

'I'll never learn,' she thought, remembering. She must accept that she was a liability to her mother, and even Tessa seemed unable to evoke her grandmother's affection.

They had travelled down by train, and were met by Dave, the odd-job man, with the brake. He greeted them warmly, and when they reached the hotel, took their bags into the hall and set them down.

There was no one about.

'Your mother's resting, I expect,' Dave had said, before

going to put the brake away. 'Miss Graham's around somewhere.'

Louise and Tessa stood in the hall and waited. Should they ring the bell on the counter, like any paying visitor, Louise had wondered, and a lump had come into her throat. For a hysterical moment she thought she was going to burst into tears, and then Ruth appeared through a door at the back of the hall.

'Louise! Well – there you are then! The train was on time, I see. Was it fun, Tessa? Had you been on a train before?' she said.

Louise had forgotten Ruth's briskness, her crackling energy.

'Ruth,' she said faintly. 'It's good to see you.'

They never kissed. It was impossible to imagine Ruth being demonstrative in any way.

'Come into the kitchen and I'll put the kettle on,' said Ruth. 'It's almost time for tea.'

They all trooped out to the kitchen, part of the extension built the year Louise left school. Long stainless steel surfaces lined the room in a clinical fashion; the cooking area was grouped in a central island. In a smaller room off the main kitchen was an old scrubbed table and some wooden chairs; this had been the original kitchen and was where the staff had their meals.

Soon Louise and Tessa were eating scones, with strawberry jam and clotted cream. There was fresh sponge cake.

Louise had finished her second cup of tea before her mother came into the room. She stood up at once.

'Mother,' she said awkwardly, and took a step forward.

'You look pale,' said her mother, not approaching. Her tone seemed to accuse. 'And Tessa. Well, child, have you no kiss for your grandmother?'

She stood waiting for Tessa to move towards her. The child glanced at Louise, who nodded, and then slid off her chair and advanced.

Mrs Hampton bent down and offered her cheek, then sat at the table herself and accepted a cup of tea from Ruth. Silence fell, as Tessa resumed her chair. Louise's appetite faded.

46

'We've been sitting for hours in the train,' she said. 'I thought we'd go down to the beach before it gets dark.'

'Take your things to your room first,' her mother instructed.

'Yes, of course,' Louise said. 'Where are we sleeping?'

They were to occupy the humblest of the double bedrooms, which overlooked the back entrance and was subject to the noise from the staff as they arrived, some on scooters, each morning.

'Won't we be able to look at the sea?' Tessa asked.

Louise had hoped they would have a front room and had allowed Tessa to share this idea. She knew that the room they had been allotted had an excellent view of the hotel's dustbins.

'I expect the hotel's too full for us to have a front room,' she said. 'You can choose which bed you'd like, Tessa.'

'Tessa will have milk and biscuits upstairs at six,' Freda Hampton had pronounced.

Louise had clasped her hands together. She had begun to tremble.

'Mother, Tessa is six and a half. Milk and biscuits isn't enough for her. She has an egg, or baked beans – something like that – for supper. I'll get it for her. We don't want to be any trouble.'

She saw herself, years ago, a little older than Tessa was now, in her attic room at the Welsh hotel which was the first home she could remember and where Ruth and her mother had met. Her mother was the cook. Louise's supper was two digestive biscuits on a thick white plate and a glass of milk, carried up on a round tin tray.

'Hmph. Does she?' her mother was saying. 'Well, she can have whatever's on the menu for entrée, and vegetables, if she wants them. I'll put it out for her. I'm not having you getting under my feet in the kitchen, Louise. You'll keep out of the way. And so will you, Tessa – out of the way of the staff and the guests.'

Tears had brimmed in Louise's eyes. She remembered creeping along the landing at that other hotel, to leave her tray at the top of the stairs for the maid to fetch. She would sit on the top step listening for sounds from below, and had once been found there, asleep, when the maid came up at nine.

'Come along, Tessa,' she said. 'We'll go and unpack. Then we'll go for a walk. Do you remember me telling you that there used to be donkeys in the field down the road? Perhaps they're still there. We'll look, on the way to the beach.'

She picked up their cases and Tessa followed her up the back staircase.

'Is Grandma pleased to see us?' Tessa had asked, helping to put garments away in a drawer. 'She seems rather cross.'

'I'm sure she's pleased,' Louise said firmly. 'But I expect she's tired. She's very busy. She's got to get dinner ready for all the people staying here.'

There were donkeys in the field and after speaking to them, Louise and Tessa went on down the cliff path to the shore. The tide was out, and the sand, grey and wetly gleaming, stretched before them, with pools and rocky outcrops here and there. Tessa ran to the water's edge, watching the wavelets lap back and forth, and then began clambering over the rocks looking for crabs. Louise followed, the tension of their journey and the anticlimax of their reception beginning to wear off as she joined in the search, slithering on the wet seaweed. In the distance, a man dug for lugworms. On the horizon, a tanker passed. Round the point was Portrinnock, the small harbour town with its fishing boats, and beyond, on the headland, the lighthouse.

It was good to be back, Louise had told herself firmly as they returned to the hotel, with Tessa running on ahead down the rough path between clumps of gorse and bracken. It was good for Tessa to run freely about without fear of cars and to breathe in this pure air. They were lucky to be able to come here for holidays, free.

Her mother had never suggested that they should return for good, after Roddy died.

'You must stand on your own feet,' she had said, after the funeral. 'I did just the same, long ago, when I was left on my own.'

Louise was still trying to do it.

Tessa was tired after the journey and was cooperative when Louise took her off early to have her bath. She came down by the back stairs, in her pyjamas and dressing gown, to have her supper.

Her grandmother put before her a perfectly poached egg, milkily opaque, sitting on a nest of spinach and surrounded by triangles of thin toast. Tessa sank her knife into the egg and caused a turgid river of yolk to flow slowly over the hill of spinach.

'Don't play, child. Eat it up,' said Freda Hampton.

'It looks so good,' said Tessa calmly, apparently undismayed at her grandmother's curt tone.

Louise had tensed at her mother's remark, ready to fly to Tessa's defence, but it wasn't necessary; the child was not at all alarmed by what Louise interpreted as an implied rebuke. She's quite tough, Louise thought, looking at Tessa with admiration.

Tessa soon disposed of the egg, and a fresh pear, which Freda had peeled for her and sliced thinly. She said goodnight to her grandmother, not offering to kiss her but holding out her hand, which Freda, looking rather surprised, clasped briefly. Louise went upstairs with her, and stayed in their bedroom reading to her for some time, until at last she could delay her own return to the adult world no longer. She was just about to go down as she was, in her jeans, when she recollected herself and turned back. Tessa expressed great surprise as she watched her put on a dress and apply a little make-up.

'Are you going to a party?' she asked.

'No. But I might help Ruth in the bar,' Louise said. 'Your grandmother always likes people to be tidy. Now, Tessa, you'll be all right, won't you, darling? The landing light is on, and if you want me I'm only just down one flight of stairs.'

'I know, Mummy,' said Tessa. 'But I won't be sick, or anything. I'll be fast asleep in a twink.'

That was the evening Louise had learned that her father might still be alive. The news had overshadowed the rest of their visit. Somewhere, an elderly man by now, he'd been living his life all these years. What did he do? On her birth certificate he was described as a clerk. Where was he now? Louise constantly wondered about him.

The days had passed quickly. Louise had helped where she could; during the slack season some of the hotel staff were laid off and Ruth was glad of help in the office where Louise understood all the work. There were a few guests, most of them casual ones staying for only a few nights while they snatched a late touring holiday. The weather, as so often in October, was good.

The morning after her abortive attempt to learn more about her father from her mother, Louise had taken the brake into Portrinnock to do the shopping. The errands done, she and Tessa had gone on foot down the hill to the jetty.

'There used to be smugglers here, long ago,' Louise had said. 'Men bringing brandy and silks and things in from France. They hid it in caves.'

'Were there pirates, too?' asked Tessa.

'Oh, probably, anchoring out at sea and coming ashore in their longboats for plunder,' Louise agreed.

There were gulls pecking at garbage in the harbour, but the tide was in and the sun shone, and it looked very pretty. A man on a ladder was painting the exterior of one of the cottages, and a woman at an easel was painting the scene. Louise and Tessa admired the handiwork of both practitioners for a while, and then walked on up the hill to the headland from where they would be able to see the lighthouse on a distant point.

A woman came out of one of the cottages on the steep hillside as they drew near. The moment she and Louise saw one another, they rushed towards each other, the woman setting down her basket to clasp Louise to her. Then she turned to kiss Tessa.

'Well, my lamb,' she exclaimed. 'Aren't you getting like your mummy? Come along in, both of you, and I'll put the kettle on while you tell me your news.'

It was Mrs Tremayne. Louise had gone to school with her sons Tom and Dick; she had spent hours, as a girl, in her small white-painted cottage.

'But you're just going out, Mrs Tremayne,' Louise said.

'Psh – what does that matter? The shopping can wait,' said Mrs Tremayne.

She had always had time, Louise remembered: time to listen; time to bind up a cut leg; time to admire a shrimp haul and boil it for tea.

Louise had allowed herself and Tessa to be shepherded into the cottage, where the walls were a foot thick and the windows small to keep out the gales. The interior was dark after the bright day outside. Tessa blinked and looked round. There was a lot of heavy furniture: big chairs, a table in the centre of the room, photographs on the mantelpiece.

Mrs Tremayne made tea in a large brown pot and poured Tessa a glass of rich, creamy milk. She cut slices of dark fruit cake for them both.

'We were talking about pirates as we came along,' said Louise.

'Plenty of them still about, fleecing the tourists,' said Mrs Tremayne. 'Not that I count your mother among them, mind, Louise. She's after the carriage trade, and why not?'

Mrs Tremayne's husband had been lost when out with the lifeboat: he'd won a medal, which was kept in a leather case on the mantelpiece. Tessa, wandering round the room with her slice of cake, looked at it with interest, and at the pictures of men in oilskins and sou'westers that hung on the wall.

'How's Tom?' Louise asked.

'Oh – doing well. In line for headmaster now,' said his mother.

At one time Mrs Tremayne had thought her elder son, Tom, and Louise might make a match. She'd had mixed feelings about it for the girl was a shy, timid little thing, not the sort to prod on an ambitious man with his way to make in the world. She needed supporting herself.

Tom had married a capable girl, but life had not been so kind to Louise, Mrs Tremayne reflected. However, she had this nice little girl, who didn't seem shy and was well-behaved, which must go down well with her grandmother. Louise had met her husband when he was staying in

Portrinnock on holiday – not at her mother's hotel but at the George in the town. The young man had thought he was on to a good thing, folk had said at the time, knowing Louise's mother had the prosperous hotel on the cliff. They'd hardly seen Louise since the wedding, and here she was now, a widow.

'I'll tell Dick you're here. He'll take you out in his boat, I expect – you'd like that, Tessa, wouldn't you?' she added, turning to the little girl, who nodded. 'Dick's always glad of a willing crew.'

'Does he still live at home?' asked Louise.

Dick, Mrs Tremayne's younger son, was a coastguard. He'd hacked off her hated plaits one day, with his penknife, while they pretended she was a damsel captured by pirates. There had been a terrible row afterwards and her mother had said that she wasn't to play with the fishermen's children. She'd kept her meetings with Tom and Dick secret, then.

'He does,' said Mrs Tremayne. She told Louise about a recent swoop by customs men and police on a yacht found to be carrying drugs. Dick had been involved with its capture, she said. The customs men and the coastguards were getting very good at detecting modern smugglers.

'It's evil,' Mrs Tremayne said. 'Drug-smuggling, I mean. It's not like a bit of brandy, which does no harm – in fact, it often does good, if you're chilled.'

Louise smiled at this liberal view. She could happily have spent the rest of the day with Mrs Tremayne, but they had to get back to the hotel with their shopping.

'Dick will be in touch,' Mrs Tremayne had promised, and he was.

Louise and Tessa went out in his boat, the *Voyager*, several times. They caught mackerel, and picked up his lobster pots. Dick talked very little and asked no questions. He showed Tessa each detail of the boat and let her take the tiller; and they went for a picnic on the last day of the visit, lighting a camp fire on a lonely beach and frying fish they had caught.

That was the night Louise found the photograph. A week later she had her first gremlin attack.

7

Lately, in the mornings, Mrs Cox had thought she was back in the nightmare time. She would wake to the dim glow from her blue bulb long before light showed at the top of the barred basement windows, and would listen for the clatter of pails and mops and shrill female voices. Her heart would flutter up into her throat with panic, and moments would pass before she remembered that those days were gone and she could walk out freely whenever she wished. No one here knew anything about it.

Mavis had saved her then. Hers was the only friendly hand extended to Mrs Cox. She'd been attacked more than once, because of her crime. There was no tolerance, in the prison, towards those who harmed children.

But she hadn't harmed Grace; she'd saved her from an immoral mother and a life of adult sin, only no one understood that, except Mavis.

Planning their fresh start, they'd decided against the country, though both would have preferred a small cottage with a garden after being confined so long. Neither was young; they'd have problems adjusting to the changed world outside, though Mavis had money waiting, her payment for services rendered. In a rural area there would be inquisitive neighbours, wanting to know all about them and perhaps, despite assumed names, somehow ferreting out the truth. Mavis, released first, had found and prepared the flat. Then, so soon, she had died, leaving Mrs Cox without the only one who had understood.

Though it was such a long time ago, Mrs Cox could remember Grace quite clearly. She was four years old, a dainty little girl with flaxen hair held back by an Alice band from her high, pure brow. She had large blue eyes. Mrs Cox had been engaged to look after the new baby, Grace's brother, when the previous nanny left to get married.

The father was in business in London, where the parents had a flat. Weekends were spent at their country house by the Thames, and in summer the children stayed all the time in the country. Not long after Mrs Cox arrived the father went on a long business trip abroad, and the mother remained in the country. She had nothing to do, and from boredom (her own explanation afterwards) or because of her own wanton nature (Mrs Cox's understanding of events) began an affair with a much younger man who lived in a boat moored further down the river. She would chug downstream in their cabin cruiser, *The Happy Maid*, and tie up alongside for their meetings. Mrs Cox had found out what was going on when she'd walked that way with the pram to feed the swans at the lock with Grace, while the baby, now sitting up, looked on.

Mrs Cox had been thoroughly shocked but had known at once where her duty lay. The mother must be taught a lesson and the child's innocence saved.

At normal times in the country, Mrs Cox's day off was at the weekend when the parents came down, but while the mother was there she went out on Thursdays, and usually took the bus to Reading. Now, Mrs Cox began to watch the mother's methods in her absence, setting out towards the bus stop as usual but returning, unseen, to the house when the cleaning woman had gone. She found that the young man spent these afternoons with the children's mother, his boat tied up at the bank beyond the lawn. The baby would be put in his cot for his nap, and Grace would play in the garden with her dolls or her tricycle. She had been taught to keep away from the river and stayed near the house.

Mrs Cox led Grace away quite easily one Thursday afternoon, taking her by the hand when she was wheeling her doll's pram through the shubbery and leading her down to the boathouse where *The Happy Maid* was berthed. Mrs Cox had given her a Mars Bar to eat, into which she had put the contents of several sleeping pills prescribed for the child's mother. Grace had been surprised by the Mars Bar, for Nanny was strict about sweets and allowed her only two after lunch each day, followed by a toothbrushing session, but she accepted that it was a special treat and surprise.

She had fallen asleep quite quickly, and Mrs Cox had hidden her limp body in the boat. She had lifted the hinged base of one of the bunks and placed the child inside the locker, comfortably arranged on a padded life-jacket. Then she had walked away along the river bank and caught the bus to Reading, where she went to the cinema, as she told the police later.

Grace was not found in time to save her. It was thought, at first, that she had wandered off and climbed into the locker, suffocating because the air in her coffin-like prison was soon used up, but the post-mortem had revealed a quantity of barbiturate in the body; enough to kill. Mrs Cox's fingerprints were found on the bottle of sleeping pills in the bathroom cupboard, and in vain did she protest that indeed, she had taken just one – without asking, true – for her own use. Witnesses agreed that she had been in the Reading cinema on the fatal day, but a bus conductor testified that she travelled on a later bus than the one she had said she had caught. She was convicted of murder.

The marriage of Grace's parents broke up soon after the hearing, and three years later the mother committed suicide, using the same brand of barbiturate that had killed her own daughter.

Mrs Cox was unrepentant. Such women did not deserve to be mothers. The world was full of women who wanted children and were denied them for one reason or another – perhaps their own natures, because to embrace a man was, to them, abhorrent. Those who misused their privilege must be punished. All small girls were potential sinners and some could be saved.

Now Mrs Cox had found another loose-living mother, and a neglectful one, too, for until lately Tessa had been left to go to and from school alone.

From behind the barred windows, Mrs Cox watched the man's legs pass as every morning Alan called at 51 Oak Way to take Tessa to school. Her mother went too, in the car. After the first week, Mrs Cox saw that the car had changed and instead of the large white one, there was a small green one that looked rather old to Mrs Cox. She would see Louise Waring and the man return, soon after nine. The man would leave, then, on foot, while the car remained parked outside. He would come back in the afternoon and spend time upstairs in the flat before he and Louise went off to meet Tessa from school. Once, walking along Oak Way pushing her wheeled shopping basket, Mrs Cox saw that Louise was driving the car.

It was really quite shameless, carrying on like that, and in broad daylight, too.

It would have to be stopped: and soon.

Now Alan had a sense of purpose again. He had plenty of time to spare from his job-hunting – all too much, in fact, since no one seemed interested enough even to interview him. He would help Louise Waring overcome her nervous attacks. You did not have to be a psychiatrist to see that she spent too much time alone, and it was certainly only natural for her to have some reaction after what she had been through. He understood her humiliation when she found out about her husband's business debts and mis-management; Alan felt humiliated too, at being rejected by Biggs and Cooper.

He soon discovered that she held a driving licence, and after a week of taking both her and Tessa to school and dropping Louise back at the flat before he went off to the library, he suggested that she should drive the green Escort with which he had replaced the Cortina. He had made quite a bit on the deal, and the Escort used far less petrol. He'd had to find some explanation for Daphne, and had told her that the Cortina was being temporarily used by one of the firm's representatives who'd piled his own car up; he'd volunteered to help out, Alan said, and Daphne believed him. It was easy to deceive someone who trusted you.

Louise took a bit of persuading to try.

'I can't,' she said. 'No, Alan.'

'Well – you needn't drive. Just sit in the driver's seat and see how it feels,' he said, getting out on the pavement so that she could slide straight across herself.

He'd been so kind; she couldn't refuse this, at least.

Louise settled down behind the steering wheel. He

helped her adjust the seat so that she could reach the controls.

'Start the engine,' he said then. 'We needn't go anywhere.'

Louise obeyed, and after they had sat there for a few minutes with the engine ticking over, Alan had looked round.

'There isn't a thing in sight,' he said. 'Why not move off? You needn't go far. Just to the next lamp post over there,' and he pointed a short distance ahead.

Louise bit her lip, put her foot down on the clutch and engaged bottom gear. With a minor jerk, they moved off. She reached the first lamp post and drove beyond it. That first day, she drove slowly along Oak Way and turned down Shippham Avenue towards the recreation ground. Then she stopped, stalling the engine, amazed at what she had managed to do but more amazed because she felt calm and as if she could do it again. Alan got her to drive round the neighbouring streets for ten minutes after that, and when he left her to do her typing while he went to the library, she was quite flushed and excited.

His own spirits fell as he wrote yet more applications for jobs. He had had only a few answers. Daphne was never curious about his mail and the formal replies he received looked to her to be simply dull business letters, which indeed they were, since almost all were to say that the posts were filled.

He went to two interviews, both for jobs that were no more than clerks' positions, and was offered one of them, but the salary was so much lower than what he had been earning, and the duties so pedestrian, with no prospects for advancement, that he turned it down. It was too soon, he thought, to settle for such a downward step, and Louise, when he told her, agreed.

It was such a relief to talk about it. She listened sympathetically to his account, each day, of the advertisements he had answered and what the employment agency had said to him – not much, as a rule – and she encouraged him not to despair. One day the right job would turn up, she assured him.

57

The day came when she drove Tessa to school by herself, just like so many other mothers who took their ability to do so for granted. Eyes shining, cheeks pink, delighted with her success, she pulled up outside 51 Oak Way, where Alan was waiting for her return.

He had been sure she would manage. She'd already driven around on her own several times. He'd leave the spare key with her, he told her, and then she could use the car to fetch her typing instead of taking a taxi, which she'd had to do, she confessed, because she couldn't cope with the bus. She'd tried, but had bad attacks each time.

He whistled cheerfully to himself, that day, walking off to the library, and stayed in good spirits until he returned in the afternoon in time to go with her to fetch Tessa from school.

But when she opened the door to his ring, he found her in tears. He had rung several times, in fact, before she answered the bell, and he had begun to wonder if she had felt brave enough to walk on ahead, for it was a lovely day with thin sunlight filtering through the bare branches of the high trees in the gardens.

'Whatever's wrong?' he asked, and hurried inside the flat where at once he put his arms around her.

Louise clung to him, shaking with sobs.

'What's wrong?' he repeated. 'There, there,' and he stroked her soft hair, as he would if the weeper had been his daughter Pauline.

Louise could not answer at first, but at last she sniffed, blew her nose on the clean handkerchief Alan gave her, as so recently he had given another to Tessa, and wiped her eyes.

'I went out this afternoon – it was such a lovely day,' she said. 'I thought I'd walk round the block on my own. But I couldn't. I got the gremlins again. I had to come back.' She'd clung to a gate, heart pounding, dizzy and sick, and had thought she would not manage to get herself home, but she had succeeded in moving just as two women, passing on the further pavement, had stopped to stare at her curiously.

'Well, never mind, Louise,' he said, though he felt deep disappointment. 'Perhaps you were bound to have some sort of set-back,' he told her, as much to reassure himself as to console her.

'It seems so silly, now, telling you,' Louise said. 'Everything's all right when you're here. I feel I could tackle anything then. You're always so calm.'

But at this moment Alan did not feel at all calm. He was still holding her, but his hands moved to her shoulders and this was not in the least like the manner in which he would comfort his daughter. It seemed, to Alan, that it was someone else, not he, who now bent his head and kissed her pale, parted lips, very gently.

She did not move, though he felt a tremor run through her. She just stood there, quietly, her eyes still full of tears.

He kissed her again, brushing her mouth softly. She stiffened within his arms, and then, lightly, he caught her upper lip between his own lips, holding it gently. The effect on Louise astonished him; she moved tight against him and her hands moved up to hold him. By the time they drew apart, gazing at each other in wonderment, Alan knew that there was more to his wish to help Louise than simple compassion.

On that sunny late winter's day, Daphne had enjoyed her game of golf in the morning. She and her partner had done quite well in their medal round, but one of their opponents, Kitty Gibson, was hitting air shots and missing easy putts and altogether having a bad time. Over lunch in the clubhouse, Kitty revealed that her husband had lost his job.

'On the scrap heap at forty-five,' she said, downing her second gin and tonic.

Her husband had held a good position in a well-established business and the Gibsons had a large house with a swimming pool. Because of the recession some hoped-for contracts had been lost and several lines of production had been cut. The axe had fallen on a number of workers, and several members of the executive staff.

A little shiver ran round the assembly of comfortably off, middle-aged middle-class women. They'd all read about cut-backs and closures, of course, but this was their first direct experience of such action. If it could happen to the Gibsons, could it not happen, also, to any of them? They did their best to put such alarming thoughts out of their minds as they tried to console Kitty.

After their good lunch, they forgot about it, settling down to the bridge tables. Kitty made it easier for them by leaving, saying she was too upset to play, and though it threw out their numbers, everyone understood.

Daphne told Alan about the Gibsons that evening. He seemed in a cheerful mood; he'd been rather quiet for the last week or two, and lately she'd wondered if he was going down with flu.

'I felt so sorry for Kitty,' said Daphne. 'Yet what can one say? I suppose there was some reason why he was sacked and not somebody else.'

'His age, I expect,' said Alan.

Here was his chance. He had only to say, 'Well, as a matter of fact it's happened to me too, but I couldn't bring myself to tell you.'

'Ridiculous,' Daphne said. 'He's like you – loyal, experienced, in his prime.' She bent to kiss his forehead, a rare gesture. 'I'm off now,' she said.

She usually stayed at home on Tuesday evenings, after a day of golf and bridge.

'Where are you going tonight?' Alan asked.

'Oh darling, I did tell you this morning, you can't have been listening,' said Daphne. 'I'm making up a four at the Manders – they always play on Tuesday and Bea Pearce can't go, she's got flu.'

'I see,' said Alan. 'Well, enjoy yourself.'

When she had gone, he went into his study and put a pile of records on – Tchaikovsky tonight, he felt in a mood for sensuous melody. While they played, he settled down to a book he had borrowed from Berbridge Central Library, about the problems of bereavement. He hoped it would help him to guide Louise along the right road to recovery. Often, while he read, his attention wandered from the book and he thought again of the kisses they had exchanged. He knew that there would be more.

*

Alan and Daphne had bought their old stone cottage in Lower Holtbury when Pauline was tiny. It had latticed windows, low ceilings, and sturdy beams holding the original part of the building together. During the years, they had added to it, building an extension in matching old stone which provided a large sitting-room and a cloakroom on the ground floor, and a new bedroom and second bathroom above. What had been the old kitchen and the dining-room had been knocked into one and was now a big kitchen, where they usually ate at a round pine table. The former sitting-room was now Alan's study, his favourite room in the house. Daphne had no musical ear, and preferred television; if they were both at home in the evening he would often retreat to his den, as Daphne called it, rather than sit through some situation comedy she wanted to watch, although he had long since developed the ability to read through almost any exterior sound.

Alan had trained a climbing Allgold rose against the front wall of the cottage, and on the lawn grew the cherry tree which gave it its name. He had laid a stone pathway round the building, and made a patio outside the french window that opened into the garden. He grew soft fruit in a cage wired against predatory birds, and in a small greenhouse he brought on seedlings and early tomatoes. He enjoyed tending the ground that he owned and saw himself as its custodian, entrusted with the duty to make it productive.

Lower Holtbury, now, was a diminishing village. The school had been closed; there was no shop, not even a post office; no inn; and no doctor, either. One of the partners in the group practice in High Holtbury held a surgery once a week in part of the former school, which was also used for occasional jumble sales, whist drives and meetings. Daphne's bridge game, that evening, was at the Manor House, the home of Gregory and Nina Manders. Gregory, until recently, had been profitably something in the city, travelling up each day in a chauffeur-driven Rolls. Now he had retired, and he and Nina had just returned from a holiday in the Bahamas. So new a recruit to the game, Daphne had not played bridge at the Manor before, but she had often been to the house when Nina Manders was chairing some charitable committee. The Manor grounds were used for various functions such as fêtes and the annual horticultural show, still held despite falling entries.

There had been very little new building in the village, and no council development for many years. Before the war, many of the cottages were the homes of farm workers; now, with mechanization, and with harvesting increasingly done by contract, a handful of workers managed the land, and most of the original labourers' cottages had been renovated. Some were occupied by couples where both husband and wife worked outside the village; some were used only at weekends; and a few, near the church – which shared its vicar with three other parishes – were owned by retired couples. These people were jealous of their rural peace and anxious to safeguard it, unlike the older village folk who could no longer cash their pensions or do their shopping close to home. Children from the village now went to school in High Holtbury.

Daphne drove to the Manor in her Mini and had an enjoyable evening. When she reached home, it was half past eleven. She saw that the bedroom light was on. Alan was probably reading, the funny old thing, she thought. All she ever read was the newspaper.

Before going to bed, she went into all the downstairs rooms to draw back the curtains. It was a chore less for the morning, though Alan didn't approve of her doing it during the winter for he said it wasted the warmth. In his study, on a table by his chair, were two books. The title of the top one caught her eye: *Problems of Death*. It must be a thriller, she thought, picking it up and glancing idly at it. *An inquiry into the aftermath of bereavement*, she read in the blurb, and saw that it came from Berbridge Central Library. The second book was about neuroses.

What on earth was he doing, reading such things? And he'd borrowed it from Berbridge, not from the Stowburgh branch library he normally used.

He wasn't ill, was he? Worrying about her, if he should die? She'd know, wouldn't she, if anything was really wrong with him? He had been rather subdued lately, it was true, but he'd eaten all his dinner this evening – every bit of the cottage pie and green beans from the freezer, followed by stewed plums, also from the garden and frozen.

Always direct, Daphne challenged him when she went into the bedroom and saw him, as she expected, sitting up in bed with a volume of poetry.

'Bit morbid, aren't you, Alan, reading those gloomy books from the library?' she said. 'Is anything wrong?'

Alan lowered the works of Walter de la Mare on to his stomach and looked at her over his spectacles.

'Not really, dear,' he said. 'I was talking to someone the other day who hadn't got over their – er – their wife's rather sudden death. Couldn't face it. I happened to be in the library checking something, and saw those books. Thought they might help.'

He had to go to Berbridge sometimes, Daphne knew, on Biggs and Coopers' business. Why not to the library? She did not query that.

'Oh – you've got them for your friend?'

'Yes – yes,' agreed Alan eagerly. How stupid of him to leave them where she'd see them, he thought.

'Who is it?' Daphne asked. 'Anyone I know?'

'No, dear. No one at Biggs and Cooper. Someone I met quite by chance,' said Alan truthfully. 'Er – Larry Walsh,' he added.

'How old is he?' asked Daphne.

'Oh – not old at all – about twenty-nine or thirty,' said Alan, guessing. 'It was a motor accident,' he added.

'Oh dear,' said Daphne. 'I suppose he's having trouble sleeping.'

'Well – yes,' said Alan. 'He – er – he has to take pills.' He supposed sleeplessness was one of Louise's problems; he didn't really know. 'He gets these attacks of giddiness when he's out.'

'Giddiness?'

'Yes. As if he's going to faint,' said Alan, various conflicting emotions of his own making him loquacious. 'Clings to the fence – has trouble getting to work, in fact. He's had a lot of time off. He hates going out at all.'

'Shock can do funny things,' said Daphne. 'It sounds a

bit like agoraphobia to me. I think that can be brought on by shock, or something like a bad illness.'

'Agoraphobia? I thought that was when you couldn't walk across a field,' said Alan.

'Well – it's fear of open spaces, isn't it?' said Daphne. 'I think it boils down to finding it hard to face life, really. Or parts of life. Not being able to meet people – cope with crowds. Emily Peters' sister had it.' Emily was a golfing friend, wife of a dentist living in High Holtbury. 'She had psychiatric treatment. I don't know if she was cured. It's horrible, I believe; the person feels really ill.'

'Maybe that's what's wrong with – er – Larry,' said Alan slowly.

'I hope you can help him,' Daphne said. 'It's like you to bother. You are a nice old thing, Alan.'

She felt very relieved to think the trouble was someone else's, and not his.

There were several books in the library which referred to agoraphobia. After doing his letters the next morning, Alan studied them, looking the subject up in the indexes and checking every reference. He became engrossed, and when he found one writer stating that sufferers could often drive themselves in cars where they could not go on foot, he felt sure that Daphne had found the answer to what was wrong with Louise. Working in a hospital as she did, she had a lot of medical knowledge.

One afternoon, a few days later, when he had had time to read quite a lot about it, he returned to the flat a little earlier than usual in the afternoon. He knew Louise had shopping to do that day; they had arranged to go to the supermarket after collecting Tessa.

Now he proposed that she should go shopping alone. She'd already delivered and collected Tessa on her own several times; it was time to be more adventurous. He'd walk on ahead, he said, and wait for her outside the supermarket. Then they'd go to the school together.

Louise agreed, though she seemed a little surprised at his suggestion.

Alan stood waiting by the wide entrance to the supermarket and watched for the car to appear. She manoeuvred it easily into a parking space near where he stood. He resisted the impulse to go over and open the door for her, for that would defeat the object of his experiment.

She smiled at him and waved. Then she got out of the car and locked the door. She turned to cross the wide pavement. Within two yards her whole demeanour had altered; she turned pale and stood still, hugging her arms to her body.

Alan was beside her at once, holding her arm.

'Breathe deeply,' he instructed. 'Just wait. You're having a panic. Hang on, it'll pass in a minute.' He'd given her much the same advice before, in this same place, without the knowledge he had now; that time, it had been just common sense. 'Don't worry,' he added. 'No one's looking. You'll be all right in a minute. Breathe deeply.'

Louise obeyed. After a few minutes her breathing steadied and her colour came back, but her eyes filled with tears.

'Oh damn, damn, damn,' she said.

Alan pressed her arm.

'Don't worry,' he said again. 'Let's do your shopping and then I'll tell you why this is happening to you.'

She seemed calm in the shop, but, not wanting to risk another attack, he kept close to her. He noticed she went to the check-out point nearest the door, confirming what he had read about agoraphobes feeling trapped and needing, in theatres or cinemas, if they managed to go to them at all, to sit by the aisle. He had thought that was an indication of claustrophobia, but in fact there seemed to be similarities between the two conditions. He knew that the affliction was a vast and complex subject, and was sure that symptoms and patients must vary immensely, but he had learned enough to feel hopeful that merely reading about it might help Louise. She had not, after all, suffered from the illness for very long, unlike many victims who endured their disability for years.

She drove the car to the school. They were early, and parked near the tree where Louise stood when she managed to walk there alone.

Alan turned in his seat to face her. Now he never thought her plain, as he had at first; he longed to banish for ever the anxious expression she so often wore. Neither, since that one occasion, had made a physical move towards the other, for both were shaken by what had happened. Alan knew that when he kissed her again it would be in no platonic fashion and a wide sea of hazard would open before them; new to that sort of intrigue, he was nervous of starting upon it, and unsure of how they would manage. He was afraid, too, of a rebuff, unaware of how deeply Louise had been stirred by the strength of her own response.

'What do you know about agoraphobia?' Alan asked her now.

'Not much,' said Louise. 'It means fear of open spaces, doesn't it? Why?'

'It's not quite as simple as that,' said Alan. 'Agora is the Greek word for market. Phobia, of course, means fear. So it really means fear of the market-place – fear of going out, fear of crowds, fear of leaving the safety of home. It can be brought on by shock,' he added. 'Like a bereavement.'

Louise stared at him.

'I think it's what's wrong with you,' he said. 'People suffering from it can get dizzy, sometimes faint, feel rooted to the spot. They get palpitations. They walk along close to fences and buildings, away from the kerb edge on pavements. Very often they're all right in cars. I've got some books about it from the library, and I found a paperback which includes it in other problems about spiders and things. You'd better read some of them yourself, Louise. See if what they say describes how you feel.'

'Can it be cured?' asked Louise.

'Of course it can,' said Alan robustly, although he had read enough to know that relief might not be easily or quickly obtained. Confidence, he felt, was the basic remedy. 'You just need some help,' he added. 'And I'm here to give it to you.'

She should really go to her doctor, he supposed; but she'd already done that, and had received only scant sympathy and tranquillizers. Alan thought that some reading could do no harm and why not see if he could help her?

If he failed, she was no worse off; already and without proper knowledge of what might be wrong, she had more confidence than when they first met.

When he found a job, he wouldn't have time.

At the prospect of no longer seeing Louise every day, Alan felt a sudden chill. He looked at her pale, thin face. She was gazing at the steering-wheel, plucking at it with her ungloved hand. There was a red scar on the back of it. He put out a finger and touched it gently.

'What's that? Did you burn yourself?' he asked.

'Mm. Stupid clot, aren't I? I knocked against the oven shelf getting something out.' She turned her hand over and slipped it into his warm, dry palm. 'Alan, if you're right, then I'm not going mad. People who are afraid of spiders, for instance, aren't mad, are they? They've just got a complex.'

'It's a phobia,' Alan corrected. 'And of course you're not mad. What an idea!' He tightened his hand round hers, feeling the little bones.

'I'd been so afraid I was losing my mind,' Louise said. 'I've tried so hard to get over it – force myself to go out. But I was getting worse and worse. Till you came along, that is. I've been so much better since then. But then today – look what happened just now. It was awful.'

'I know,' said Alan. 'But one of the books I've been reading says that people with most phobias go into a sort of panic. It's what you call your gremlins. Say it's spiders you don't like – you mentioned them yourself. You know how they often appear in the bath, they come up the drain.' There were a lot of spiders at Cherry Cottage; they lived in the thatch. Pauline had never cared for them and Alan had often rescued them from the bath in response to her cries. He thought it unlucky to kill them.

Louise agreed that spiders did seem to enjoy looking for water in bath outlets.

'Well then – you're a spider hater, we'll say, so every time you go into the bathroom you're expecting to see one, and you're tense and alarmed in advance. So when you do see the spider, you get into a panic. But if you just hung on for a minute, breathed deeply and let the panic – or

67

gremlins – pass, you could probably cope. You could run the spider out with some water, for instance, or trap it in a glass, put some paper over the end and throw it out of the window. You're much bigger than it, after all, and I don't think there are many tarantulas in this country.'

They both laughed at this.

'And you think agoraphobia can be tackled like spiders?' said Louise.

'I don't see why not,' said Alan. 'I bet, today, you sub-consciously thought as you got out of the car, "Oh dear, now I've got to cross the pavement and I felt funny here the other day," so that in a way you were expecting trouble.'

'I wondered why you hadn't come up to the car,' Louise admitted. 'I was wishing you had. But now I see you did it on purpose, didn't you?'

'Well, yes.' He pressed her hand. 'The children are coming out,' he said. 'I'll leave you some of these books and I'll see what else I can find out about it. Then we'll talk about what we can do. Maybe you should see what your doctor says, but I can't see that delaying for a bit will make much difference.'

He went back to tea with them. He always did that now. Louise had made a chocolate cake. Afterwards, until it was time for Alan to go home, they played Ludo.

Mrs Cox had seen them all come in together. At least, she had seen the legs passing her basement window. She watched for them now, every day, her chair pulled comfort-ably forward: the grey worsted legs with the well-shined black shoes; the long black boots; and the little white socks with the brown zip ankle boots below. The two adult pairs of legs went in and out too often without the third pair: each afternoon the man arrived alone and was up there in that flat with Louise before they both went to the school. There was only one meaning to that. Louise was a fast woman, and a stupid one, too, in Mrs Cox's opinion; men were only after one thing, like the young man in the boat so long ago, and it was foolish, as well as wicked, to let them turn your head, as Grace's mother, and now Louise, had done. Tessa, if not prevented, would do it too, in time.

68

Mrs Cox had a baby-sitting appointment that night at the Duncans' house, just round the corner in Shippham Avenue. Mr Duncan fetched her as usual, though it was no distance at all to walk. As she sat in the well-furnished sitting-room of Beech House, while the baby slept upstairs, Mrs Cox thought about what must be done. While she reflected, she knitted a small cardigan destined for the Duncans' baby, now six months old.

The baby began to cry at half-past nine. He did not stop quickly, so after a while Mrs Cox went up to see what was wrong; she never went at once; they often dropped off again if you left them. The child was probably teething.

Mrs Cox spoke briskly to the infant and changed his wet nappy. Then she picked up the bottle of sedative medicine used by the mother if the child refused to settle, and left handy in case it was needed. Mrs Cox poured out the requisite dose and the baby drank it down without demur. It was pleasant to take, it seemed, though it took a little time to work. Mrs Cox, however, never pandered to any baby that was in her care. She tucked the child firmly back into his cot and left the room. There were a few small whimpers, but soon there was silence. The mixture would be effective with an older child, too, if a large enough dose was given, and it could be bought over the counter at any chemist's. Reinforced with a sleeping pill or two, to induce quicker action, and mixed with cocoa and plenty of sugar, it would be easy to get Tessa to swallow it. Her wicked mother deserved to suffer, and a chance would come, as it had with Grace. Grace, the sweet innocent child, had been protected for ever from sin; Tessa should be made safe too.

In Mrs Cox's medicine cupboard, high on the bathroom wall, was a big bottle half-full of chloral hydrate prescribed for Mavis, who had often been nervy, restless and disturbed. It had had a magic effect, swiftly ensuring profound sleep for many hours. There was also a bottle of large white sleeping tablets which Mavis had taken regularly.

Mrs Cox never took drugs herself, but she'd kept these after Mavis died, for you never knew what you might one day need. A mixture might be best for Tessa.

8

While Mrs Cox was baby-sitting round the corner, Louise settled down with the books which Alan had left. The radio was tuned to a classical concert, and with Mozart and Brahms forming a soothing background, she discovered her symptoms described with frightening accuracy. Instant relief swept over her as she read on; she was not insane, nor was she simply feeble. She had a genuine illness.

There were various cures, she learned, including group therapy and analysis, even the use of tape recordings which, it seemed, could be quietly played to provide encouragement as the sufferer undertook an expedition beyond the safe bounds of home. Louise read about the onset of panic she knew so well and that Alan had mentioned. Accept it and let it pass, the book advised, just as he had said. Already, since meeting Alan and without considering his theory, she was feeling better. Her own improvement was reflected in Tessa, who was eating more and had lately earned one gold and two silver stars at school. She hadn't made the school journey alone for some time now; she was much too young for the burden of supporting her mother, as she had done until Alan came into their lives.

Louise thought back to her own childhood and the hotel in Wales with her small attic room. She had been frightened of shadows cast by the beams which crossed it. She was terrified when, one night, a bat flew in and swooped over her bed. She hid under the bedclothes, screaming, but no one heard her and her screams turned to sobs until at last she fell asleep, exhausted. In the morning, the bat had gone.

One theory Louise read of implied that a shock sustained in childhood and possibly forgotten could be revived by some later trauma and provoke a subsequent phobia.

Bats in your bedroom, in childhood, weren't enough, surely, she thought, and laughed at the idea as she dismissed it. Perhaps, since she'd forgotten so much – could remember nothing, really, until the hotel in Wales – there was some hidden horror. Perhaps it was connected with the departure of her father?

At intervals through the weekend, Louise thought about him. How different things might have been, she thought, if he had stayed in her life. But what sort of man had be been? Was he like Roddy? Or was he a man like Alan – gentle and kind? Her days were so different now, with his friendship. Often, she thought of the kisses they had exchanged which were so different from any she had known before, and which had come about in so natural a manner. All her instincts had been to prolong the moment. He hadn't mentioned a wife, and she hadn't asked; a man like that had to be married, though, and in time he would tell her about it.

He did, on Monday.

After taking Tessa to school they both hurried back to Oak Way, for they wanted to discuss the books which Alan had left with her over the weekend.

'It's like being reborn, Alan,' Louise told him. 'I feel so grateful to you. I slept like a log last night, and without any pills.'

'It shows,' Alan said. 'You look splendid.'

They were in the kitchen. Louise had put the kettle on, and now, as she turned to spoon instant coffee into mugs, he caught her by the shoulders and turned her gently round. Softly he kissed her mouth, then let her go. Louise turned back to the mugs and made their coffee. They sat down at the table, smiling at one another.

'Let's take the day off,' Alan said. 'The sun's coming out – let's have a day in the country.' He shut his mind to the thought of the employment agency and the newspapers that waited in the library. 'Why not?' he urged.

Louise had a pile of typing that had to be done to a deadline. She thought of the job which one day, perhaps very soon, Alan would get, and which would end what had barely begun between them. For once she felt no compulsion to flee from a positive act. She could do the typing at night, when Tessa had gone to bed.

'Good idea,' she said.

She drove. She was improving all the time. They went through the town and headed westwards into the country, where if it wasn't too cold they could walk on the downs. The wind was chilly, but the sun was shining and there were only small, puffy clouds in the pale blue sky. There was, at last, the feeling of spring in the air as they parked the car and got out. The wind caught at them as they set off up a track towards a small copse on the top of a hill. Alan took her hand and put it in his pocket with his own. They walked in silence for a while, until Louise said, 'Tell me about your wife. You are married, aren't you?'

He did not answer at first, tightening his grasp on her hand and staring down at their two sets of feet trudging over the turf.

'Yes,' he said at last. 'Daphne and I have always got on well.' But with her he'd never felt the sense of elation that filled him now, walking along with this frail young woman who somehow reminded him of a wounded bird, whose hand in his was so small and thin. 'We've got one daughter who's married and lives near York.' He did not mention the baby.

'Your wife doesn't know you're out of a job, does she?' said Louise.

'No,' Alan said, and added, 'It must seem very strange to you that I haven't told her.'

'It doesn't,' Louise replied. She knew about non-communication. She hadn't known about Roddy's work. 'You probably didn't want to worry her,' she suggested.

'In a way, yes,' Alan agreed, glad of this excuse which he knew was not the whole truth. 'But also, you see, she's always so busy and on the go. It's hard to catch her in a settled moment. I intended to tell her but the chance kept passing and after a while it seemed too late altogether. I've decided, now, to wait until I've found something.'

'And you're leaving home at your usual time and getting back when you always did?'

'Yes.' Admitting it, Alan felt sheepish. How craven it must seem.

'Mightn't she telephone you at the office?'

'She hasn't for years,' said Alan.

Louise did not seem to think this strange.

'It's my good luck, then,' she said, in a firmer voice than he had ever heard her use. 'I'll have to get cured quickly before you start a new job. I won't be able to manage it on my own.'

He kissed her again then, her face cold in the wind.

'You won't have to,' he said, and wanted to add, you need never be quite alone again, yet caution compelled him to leave the words unsaid: better not promise something you might be unable to deliver. He kissed her once more, holding her close, his mouth gentle at first and then more demanding. Slowly, she relaxed and then he felt her respond.

They walked on at last, their hands linked.

Two nights later, when Daphne was playing bridge, Alan went round to Oak Way, bringing with him a bottle of wine. Tessa had gone to bed, and Louise was expecting him, for he'd suggested this plan that afternoon and she had agreed.

She'd changed, and was wearing a dark red dress. Her hair was newly washed, and a flowery fragrance came from her as he bent and lightly kissed her lips when she opened the door.

They sat on the sofa at first, drinking their wine, and Alan moved close to her. When he gently moved on from kissing her to begin soft, tender caresses, a wild delight took hold of Louise and any last fear, any lingering thought of resistance, was gone. She could not bear to release him.

She was shy at first, like an untried girl, and she enchanted Alan, who had forgotten, in Daphne's familiar and always welcoming arms, that women were not all the same.

Before he left her, he made tea and brought it to her in bed, where they drank it together.

'Fancy tea in bed in the night!' Louise exclaimed, the sheet drawn up round her naked breasts. 'I didn't know this sort of thing happened – that it could be so much fun.'

'Didn't you?' Alan asked. He drew the sheet down and kissed her, and Louise shivered with pleasure.

She shook her head. Her hair, loosed from its customary clasp, fell across her face. She didn't know how to describe Roddy's untender invasion.

'I didn't like it,' she said, and added simply, 'I just used to wait for it to be over.'

Alan, the expectant grandfather, could not wait to gather her up in his arms again. There'd just be time, if he drove home fast, before Daphne returned.

Mrs Cox was still up when he left. She'd been indulging herself that evening, looking at her cuttings book, and she'd heard him arrive earlier, his brisk stride on the path. She'd been listening since then, waiting for him to go. Her hearing wasn't as good as once it had been, but she opened the living-room window a fraction and she heard soft voices as Louise said goodbye at the top of the iron stairs.

The shameless hussy, Mrs Cox thought, putting her cuttings book back in its drawer and glancing up at her clock. It was shocking.

Daphne wouldn't notice his car was still warm when she put her own Mini away beside it, Alan thought, hurrying into Cherry Cottage some time later. He felt deliciously languid.

He went into his study to put on a record. Tchaikovsky again, it had to be, he thought, after all that. It had been wonderful, and his heart, literally, seemed to sing as he listened to *Romeo and Juliet*. He was dozing a little when he heard Daphne's key in the door, and the record was still playing, but when she came in to say she was back he appeared to be reading.

'How's Larry Walsh getting on?' Daphne asked, as they made ready for bed. 'Have you seen him again?'

Who on earth was Larry Walsh? Alan stared at Daphne, and was on the point of asking her whom she meant when, just in time, he remembered his fictitious friend with Louise's initials in whom Daphne had diagnosed agoraphobia.

74

'Oh – he's more cheerful,' he said.

'I asked Emily about her sister,' Daphne said. 'It seems she's not completely cured, though she's much better. She's going to group therapy classes where they all talk about it, and then are taken for escorted walks and so on, gradually going further, and on buses and that sort of thing.'

'I suppose cases vary,' said Alan cautiously. It was worth continuing this conversation; Daphne might produce useful information.

'Some people don't leave their homes for years,' Daphne said. 'They bring up their children like that. Amazing, isn't it?'

Alan remembered a case history he had read. He said that Larry had no trouble driving the car, and was all right once he reached his office.

'Well, he knows what caused it, doesn't he?' Daphne said. 'It was losing his wife. I expect he'll get over it in a year or two. Someone was saying at the hospital that it takes three years to recover from a bereavement.'

'Some people never recover,' said Alan.

'Well, they adjust,' said Daphne. 'You can get used to anything, if you have to. It's like losing a leg – dreadful. But you have to learn to walk again. You're not the same, but you can live normally. Or try to. It's like that after any serious illness, in fact. You can't put the clock back and pretend it never happened.'

'You see a lot of surface healing, don't you?' he said.

'Yes. Brave people learning to walk and talk and dress themselves after strokes and terrible accidents,' Daphne said. 'Sometimes their families don't realize what huge efforts they have to make.'

What a good woman Daphne was, Alan thought. Yet if anyone told her that, she would be embarrassed and would brush the tribute aside. She was calm and confident, but her personal courage had never been challenged. Her health had always been good; she had had loving parents and a secure childhood. He was not, himself, the world's most dynamic man, but until tonight he had been her faithful partner and had provided for her, gladly, always hoping for her happiness, for almost a quarter of a century.

Was he insulting her, now, by seeking to spare her from worry? She would, he knew, support him in whatever might lie ahead, if he gave her the chance.

She had just said, herself, that one could not put back the clock. It was too late, and tonight he had taken a step down another path which he meant to explore to the end. He couldn't give up Louise. He was counting the minutes already until he would see her again.

Creaming her face, Daphne told him that her golfing friend, Kitty Gibson, had given up playing. Her husband still hadn't found a job and was very depressed; they had put their house up for sale. Daphne thought the real reason she'd stopped going up to the golf club, where her subscription was valid for the rest of the year, was because she dreaded facing her friends.

Alan was rather surprised that she should show so much perception.

9

On Friday morning, Mrs Cox went to the shops. She had seen the legs go past as usual; the two pairs from the flat first, the mother and daughter, then later the other two pairs, the mother again and the man. When Mrs Cox left, pushing her wheeled shopping basket, the old green car was outside 51 Oak Way, but it had gone by the time she returned.

Mrs Cox had been to the supermarket to buy a chop and some vegetables for her midday meal. In the evening she ate lightly – an egg, poached or boiled, with toast and tea, or cheese on toast, though sometimes that made her dream. When she went baby-sitting, a meal was always provided – a casserole in the oven, or a tastefully arranged salad – and a glass of sherry or wine. Sometimes there would be a fresh peach, or a pear, or even strawberries and cream. At one house a note would advise her to help herself to yoghurt from the refrigerator as her dessert, but Mrs Cox didn't care for that new-fangled stuff. She preferred a nice rice pudding, or custard, or old-fashioned junket made properly with essence of rennet.

After the supermarket, she went to the chemist's for Steradent for her dentures, a bottle of baby oil with which to combat the dryness of her elderly skin, and some of the sedative medicine her various employers used to soothe their fractious children at night. The girl in the chemist's shop took scant notice of who bought these items; she was used to grandmothers buying nursery requirements.

Mrs Cox took the mixture back and put it in the medicine cupboard. A child of six would need a very large dose to fall unconscious, and it did not work at once. She would have to use something that acted quickly. She looked at the bottle of chloral hydrate, and the flat white tablets. They'd have the same effect, she was sure, as the blue pills she had used long ago.

She drew some chloral hydrate out of the bottle with an ear dropper and squeezed the liquid into a hole she had made in the base of a Mars Bar. Three times she filled the dropper and added its contents to the caramel mixture. She plugged the hole with chocolate and lit a match to melt it a little so that the drug was contained and her tampering concealed, though a child never looked closely at titbits.

Tessa would bite greedily into it, swallow it down too fast to notice the bitterness, as Grace had eaten, long ago, a Mars Bar prepared the same way with another drug.

She put it in her handbag. In the past she had often met Tessa when, on fine days, she had walked in the recreation ground and the child had been coming back from school. Mrs Cox liked watching the children playing. She would talk to the mothers sometimes as they pushed toddlers on the swings or stood by the slide or the see-saw. Mrs Cox's charges had all had swings in their own gardens; there was none of this communal playing for them, though selected friends had come to tea and to parties. But times had changed.

Lately, Tessa had not come this way at all. Her mother, and that man, her mother's friend, had been meeting her at the school. Why was he not at work? Why had he time to spend half the afternoon in the flat with the child and her mother? For he never left until half-past five.

The afternoon was sunny and dry. Mrs Cox had a nap after lunch and then, just before three, she set off for a stroll. She sat on a bench near the gate through which Tessa would come on her way home from school if today was to be the day.

One day, she would come through it alone, and today might be the one. They would sit together, Mrs Cox planned, and when the Mars Bar was eaten they would walk to the river. Tessa would go where Mrs Cox led; children always obeyed her. She was not allowed to go to the river alone, of course, so it would be quite a treat. When she felt drowsy, Mrs Cox would find her somewhere to rest. No one would query a child and an elderly woman seen together, the child leaning against the woman as if with affection. When the moment came, with no one in sight, it would be easy to slip the child into the water. Later, when enough time had passed and the small body had quite disappeared, Mrs Cox would raise the alarm and be found in distress on the bank. They had been walking together, she would say – she could not say that Tessa had been on the path without permission, since they would have been noticed; she had run on and slipped.

What would Louise Waring say then, wondered Mrs Cox with grim satisfaction as she brooded over her plan.

But that fine, sunny day, Louise and Tessa came together through the recreation ground gate. Together they went to the swings, where for quite ten minutes the small girl enjoyed herself. Hand in hand, they went on home.

They never noticed that Mrs Cox was there, watching them, holding her leather bag on her lap, the Mars Bar inside it. They loitered a little. Alan had been for an interview and would not be back just yet.

Alan's interview that day was at Coxwell, with a light engineering firm of repute, whose products and processes would be easy for him to understand.

Setting out for the appointment, his heart was light. If he

got the job, he could tell Daphne the truth about his redundancy but let her think he was still working out his notice. He could see Louise in the evenings, while Daphne was out. There would be plenty of chances for them to meet. He whistled, driving along. Things were improving, he thought, driving into the small town with plenty of time to spare before his appointment.

He parked in a side road and went for a stroll down the main street. There were the usual branches of multiple stores as in most towns now, but there were plenty of other shops too, including a record shop that had some musical instruments in the window. He went inside.

Browsing among the stock, he found *Peter and the Wolf* and on impulse bought it for Tessa; Louise had a record player, her own property, she said, during her marriage, and she had been able to prove it by producing the bill, so she'd kept it and a good many records too.

He asked if they sold recorders. They did, though only treble ones. He bought two, one each for Louise and Tessa. It wasn't the flute she had once wanted, but he knew she would find it a lot easier to play, and the two could have fun together.

From a florist's near the music shop, he bought six bunches of daffodils, and walked jauntily back to the car with his shopping, which he put on the back seat. Then he drove off to keep his appointment.

The Escort looked very inferior, so shabby and so old, inserted into a space in the visitors' parking lot between a large Peugeot and a BMW. There was a Datsun, too, and a Honda. When he went into the office building and was directed to a room where several men were already silently waiting, two smoking, one gazing at the ceiling and one reading the *Guardian*, he spent some time wondering which man belonged to which vehicle.

At last his turn came to enter the interview room.

Alan tried to look confident, sitting before the three directors who were assessing him. His qualifications for the job and his experience were what had got him thus far; now he must try to impress them with his good sense and adaptability.

They kept him some time, longer than the much younger man who had gone in ahead of him and who had come out wearing a somewhat complacent smile beneath his droopy moustache.

Louise and Tessa were delighted with the recorders and the flowers and with *Peter and the Wolf*.

'So many!' exclaimed Louise, arranging the daffodils in two different vases.

'A golden portent for the future,' said Alan poetically.

He felt very happy. He had known a great armful of flowers would please her more than an azalea, or forced irises which would soon wither. The little room looked as if it had been invaded by sunlight.

Louise wanted to know all that had happened at the interview, and when he told her, said she was sure he had said the right things and that he would get the job. Alan, himself, was hopeful; he had left the room with a feeling the men talking to him had liked him.

'You've done well, too,' he said.

She had. She had walked to school and met Tessa without the slightest sign of her gremlins.

When Alan left, both felt the weekend stretching ahead as a vast gulf, but both knew he would come round again in the evening as soon as he could.

His chance came on the following Monday, and again on the next Wednesday. He skipped Thursday, when Daphne was out again, but it seemed a shame to miss Friday, too, with another weekend ahead.

Mrs Cox, down below, noted it all and waited. She'd find Tessa alone one day in the end.

Daphne was helping at a jumble sale in the village on that Saturday afternoon. Alan spent the afternoon doing odd jobs in the garden and was having a cup of tea in the kitchen when Daphne came in, bursting with news.

Kitty Gibson's out-of-work husband had committed suicide the previous night. It seemed that he had taken some of Kitty's sleeping pills, thoughtfully waiting to do it until she was asleep herself. Then he had crept out of bed and gone downstairs to swallow them with, it appeared, a great deal of whisky. Kitty had found him in the morning, dead in a chair by the electric fire, which still burned. A note was beside him.

Alan felt icily chill.

'Poor bastard,' he said.

'Kitty will get no insurance,' said Daphne. 'You don't, if it's suicide – or so people were saying. What a cowardly thing to do.'

'He must have felt very discouraged,' said Alan. 'Hopeless, really, trudging round applying for jobs and being passed over for younger men. No doubt that's what had been happening,' he hastily added.

'He was feeble,' said Daphne. 'He must have been to give up so soon.'

Alan turned away. It was only meeting Louise, he felt, that had saved him from total despair, though he hoped he would never take that way out. But one day his own moment of reckoning might have to be faced.

10

In Alan's car, Louise drove carefully through Berbridge on Monday afternoon. She reached the municipal multistorey car park and circled her way round its floors till she found an empty slot near the top. She didn't enjoy driving up the ramps with another car close behind, and when she had parked and switched off the engine she sat for some seconds, waiting, in case one of her attacks came on, but it didn't, so she got out of the car and locked it, then went off along the walkway to the main street. She passed Boots and Marks and Spencer and crossed the road by the town hall, where she turned into a side street. Here the typing agency had its office on the third floor of a tall building. Louise felt cheerful and confident now; she wouldn't have an attack for ages, she decided, if ever again. She stayed for a cup of coffee and received a new script. Walking away, she still felt compelled to keep close to the shops, away from the kerb, but that was a rational thing to do; there was less chance of being run over on the inside, she told herself, walking on swift feet to meet Alan with a delicious, excited flutter inside her.

She hated it when he left the flat to go home. Already his embrace was familiar. To her, it was strange that so large a man could be so tender. He brought with him a sense of warmth and security such as she had never known before, and Louise saw no reason why their affair should end, for even after he found a new job he could come round in the evenings when his wife was out; she went out a lot.

Louise had learned a good deal about Daphne. Alan had talked about her now, and she pictured a brisk hearty woman, in tweed trousers for golf, striding about like a human bulldozer regardless of people's feelings. Yet from the way he spoke, he seemed very fond of her.

Louise knew that Alan loved her, too; she didn't really see how you could love two women at the same time but supposed they were different sorts of emotion. Very likely he and his wife hadn't made love for years, she thought. She hurried on through the town, eager to join him. They would go together to fetch Tessa from school, almost as if she had a father again.

A father: Louise herself had one now. She had been preoccupied with the idea of him until Alan had come into her life and driven out of her mind what was becoming almost an obsession. Now, that unknown man entered her thoughts once more. Her footsteps slowed as the familiar questions repeated themselves in her head.

She had to go past the car park to get to the library, where Alan would be, and all of a sudden the papers she carried felt heavy. Louise turned off to put them in the car; it was pointless to drag them round with her.

She placed them on the back seat of the Escort, and as she re-locked the door she noticed a Mini hovering, the driver apparently waiting to see if she was going to leave a free space.

Louise shook her head, and after a moment the Mini

moved on. In it was Daphne, with Kitty Gibson. They had
come to Berbridge to buy a dark coat for the inquest on
Charles Gibson and for his funeral. Kitty had only bright-
coloured clothes, for those were what he had liked her to
wear.

Louise walked on to the library, where Alan was sitting,
as he had said he would be, in his usual place near the
Encyclopaedia Britannica.

She was still thinking about her father.

That evening, Daphne said, 'I thought I saw someone
trying to steal something out of your car today, Alan.'

'Oh?' Alan looked up from the crossword which he was
trying to finish. What was coming?

'In the multistorey park in Berbridge,' Daphne went on.
'A woman. She'd got the door open and was leaning in
towards the back. But she shut the door and walked away
with just her handbag, so I didn't ask her what she was
doing.'

Alan was sitting bolt upright with shock, but he thought
swiftly.

'It was the new girl from the office,' he said smoothly.
'The one taking over from Stephanie. She'd taken my car to
go on an errand – something rather urgent cropped up.'
While he spoke, Alan continued to gaze at the crossword.

'Oh,' said Daphne. 'Is she nice? Efficient?'

'Very,' said Alan. 'Her name is Louise.'

It was lovely to say it like that, let the soft sound of her
pretty name hang in the air.

'That's good,' Daphne said. 'I'm sorry you couldn't
persuade Stephanie to stay, though. Changes are tiresome.'

'What were you doing in Berbridge?' Alan asked. She
rarely went there; her patients were all from the Stowburgh
area.

Daphne explained about Kitty.

'I took the afternoon off,' she said. 'I'll make the time up
some other day. It was worrying Kitty. We got a dark
raincoat at Marks – quite smart. It'll be useful for years so
it wasn't money wasted. Kitty didn't want to borrow
anything; besides, nothing I've got would fit her.'

What if she'd been a bit later and seen him and Louise return to the car from the library? Louise had been quiet at first but by the time they reached the car park she'd been laughing, and as they walked together in the dank interior of the building he'd taken her hand. The idea shook Alan. He'd thought Berbridge was safe.

'Poor Kitty's in a terrible state,' Daphne said. 'I hope she doesn't go phobic, like that friend of yours. I asked her to stay with us for a while but she wouldn't agree. I don't think it's at all good for her to be alone at the moment.'

Phew, Alan thought. Thank goodness Kitty had not accepted, for with Daphne out such a lot, he'd have been left on his own with the widow. But how nice women were to each other, he reflected, how steady their friendships. It was unfortunate that Louise seemed to have no long-standing female friend, not even, as far as he could understand, one from her childhood days.

'You were quite right to ask her, Daphne,' he said, writing in BUSINESS AS USUAL at number 5 down in the crossword.

The next morning, Alan received a letter from the firm in Coxwell to say that they could not offer him the position for which he had been interviewed.

Alan had taken the letter into the lavatory with him, so that he could read it without delay and without Daphne being curious about any reaction he might show.

Sick disappointment filled him. He had allowed himself to become quietly confident that he would be appointed and now he felt real physical distress. Sweat broke out on his forehead and his heart pounded. This was what Kitty Gibson's unfortunate husband had experienced, perhaps many times: this build-up of hope and then the bitterness of a new rebuff.

He rinsed his face with cold water and dried it carefully, then emerged with a bright smile to put Daphne's golf clubs in her car and wish her a pleasant day.

Louise noticed at once that something was wrong although Daphne hadn't, Alan thought – irrationally, for he had tried very hard not to let her. With Louise there was no need to be guarded.

'They're fools at that firm,' Louise said, with passion, when he told her. 'Fancy passing you up.'

'I expect they took one of the younger men,' Alan said. It would have been that smug one with the drooping moustache, he decided.

During the days that followed, he tried to put this fresh rejection out of his mind, but it had been a real blow. While he was with Louise and Tessa, he was able to forget the nagging anxiety, but driving in and out each day, and at home, the worry pressed hard.

On Thursday, Alan went for another interview, arranged by the agency. The firm made electronic games and puzzles, which Alan thought pointless, and he did not take to the man who interviewed him, or the girl with bleached hair, a slit skirt and stilt heels, who admitted him to the office. He was told that the firm was progressive and the staff, on the whole, young; what was lacking was business experience which he could supply. He thought, irritably, that they wanted some sort of father-figure to lean on, and would not only milk his knowledge but probably make use of his contacts, too. When they'd done all that, they'd cast him aside without a qualm. Yet if he were offered the job, he would have to consider accepting it; the fate of Charles Gibson had shaken him.

Daphne herself lived as nearly as possible from day to day; she was not one to anticipate bridges she might never encounter, except on behalf of her patients. Her work was going well that week; old Mrs Burt had settled in at her son's, and the daughter-in-law, whom Daphne and the health visitor had felt some concern for, had begun to think of finding a part-time job. The extra money would help the household generally, and the daughter-in-law might as well make the most of her opportunity before, as must surely one day happen, the old lady fell ill again.

Kitty Gibson took up some of Daphne's time that week. A verdict of suicide while the balance of the mind was disturbed was brought in at the inquest, and the funeral was arranged for the following Monday at noon.

'Will you go to the office first?' Daphne asked.

'What? When?' Alan frowned. What was she talking about?

'Charles Gibson's funeral,' said Daphne. 'You're coming, of course.' How vague Alan seemed to be getting these days, she thought; it was often hard to get his attention but then he'd always been rather a dreamer. 'Well?' she prompted.

'I must go in first,' Alan said. 'I'll meet you there, shall I? At the crematorium.' He wouldn't miss seeing Louise.

11

He was up there again this evening. It was disgusting.

Mrs Cox was keeping a tally of the visits that man with the green car paid to Louise Waring.

Gone was her original concern for Tessa's physical well-being; anger at the moral danger facing the child was now predominant in her mind. The pair's conduct was brazen. Had they no shame, indulging in their goings-on right under the nose of the child? Mrs Cox muttered away to herself, peering out from behind the curtain to watch Alan's legs go by.

By eleven, he still had not gone. He had never been so late before. Could she have missed him? It was possible, for she had had to go to the bathroom, and had been to her bedroom to switch on the electric blanket.

Mrs Cox was so curious that she put on her coat and went out, up her own steps out of the basement well and along the path to the road, to see if his car was still there. It was: the green car with the dent in the wing and the M registration.

She was quite out of breath with distress when she reached her own flat again and she sat in her chair for a while, brooding. Then she got up and looked at her bottle of baby sedative. She unwrapped the prepared Mars Bar and inspected it. There were the tablets, too, the large flat white ones which Mavis had used till the end.

Against one wall of Mrs Cox's living-room was an old oak chest, once Mavis's; it had a hinged lid, like the bunk in *The Happy Maid*, that cruiser where Grace had lain sleeping so sweetly, the last sleep of death. Mrs Cox raised the lid. Inside was a folded rug; nothing else.

The child would be well concealed in the chest, Mrs Cox decided, safely sleeping while she planned how to move her when the time arrived to put her scheme into action.

She mustn't delay. Tessa's soul was in mortal danger.

She looked at her large, wheeled wicker shopping basket and wondered if the child could be moved in that, and decided, regretfully, that Tessa was too big to be placed inside it.

She would need something else. The wheelbarrow Terence Henshaw used for his gardening, with a rug thrown over the child's unconscious form?

She thought about it, sitting there waiting for Alan to pass the window, and still he did not leave the upstairs flat.

When he arrived at the flat that morning to take Tessa to school Alan had had an air of suppressed excitement, but Louise did not learn the reason for it until the afternoon when he returned from the library. He came in hung about with parcels, and unwrapped them in the kitchen. He'd brought a bottle of wine, some smoked salmon, steak, and a pineapple.

'What is all this?' Louise had said, laughing. 'Is it your birthday?'

'It's a celebration,' said Alan. 'I can stay the night – that is, if I may,' and he had caught her to him, covering her face with small, light kisses.

'Really?' Louise would not ask why; there were areas of his life that he might not want to discuss.

'Yes, really,' said Alan. He released her, and turned away so that she should not see his face. 'Daphne's gone away to visit our daughter for a few days,' he said.

After Charles's funeral, Pauline had telephoned. Her husband was going to a conference in Cambridge and she hadn't been feeling very well. She didn't want to be on her own so Daphne had cancelled her golf – luckily it wasn't a match and her partner was understanding – and had set off this morning for York. She and Alan had rarely been separated before. He'd telephoned her to make sure she'd arrived safely, going home to do it during the afternoon and collecting his shaving kit. Louise never asked him awkward questions and he knew she would express no curiosity about why he had not left the car in Oak Way as usual that morning, if, indeed, she had noticed.

'I see,' said Louise softly. 'How lovely.'

Daphne was not due back until Friday; they could have three whole nights together.

The next morning Alan went back to Cherry Cottage to pick up the mail and a clean shirt; he'd forgotten to stop the milk, and he took the bottle in. It was probably better not to cancel it, he thought, since Daphne might query the reduced bill. He telephoned her before leaving the house, and as on the day before, she thought he was ringing from the office. Then he rang the employment agency in Berbridge, and was told of a possible job. The agency had mentioned him to the firm, which was on the other side of the county; they wanted to see him and he should lose no time in pursuing it, he was advised.

Alan telephoned and made an appointment for Friday afternoon. Then he drove to Oak Way to collect Louise and take her to lunch at a pub on the river. They went straight back to Oak Way; it was like a honeymoon.

That evening their dinner was Louise's surprise. She had slipped out in the morning to shop, while Alan was away with the car. Elation buoyed her along; she had no onset of gremlins. They had melon, pork chops in a cider sauce, and apricot fool, eating at the small round table in the sitting-room. There were tall yellow candles, and a tiny vase of crocuses out of the garden.

Later, in bed, Louise said, 'Alan, you've done so much for me. I'm very happy – very lucky. But I haven't forgotten about my father. I still want to know more about him.'

'You do?' Alan could sympathize with her view. If he

88

had discovered, in adult life, that his own father, thought to be dead, was alive, he would want to see him too.

'Mm.'

'What do you want to do?' he asked.

'Find him. I must, Alan – or find out what's happened to him. He keeps coming into my mind,' she said. 'I think about you quite a lot,' she added, tugging gently at the hairs on his chest. 'But not all the time. How do I start to search?'

Alan sighed. He wished she would leave it; but perhaps, if she satisfied her curiosity, she would then come to terms with her early life.

'Where were you born?' he asked.

'In London, I think,' she said.

'Your birth certificate will tell you,' he pointed out. 'And give your parents' address at the time. You could start there.'

'It's in the sideboard,' she said, and wanted to get it then, but he wouldn't let her, stopping her with kisses.

He was asleep first, and when she heard him breathing evenly, Louise slipped out of bed and from the room. She opened the sideboard drawer and took out the envelope containing her papers. There was the birth certificate, and it showed an address in Putney. She wrote it down, put the certificate back in the drawer and went back to bed.

That night, sleep was elusive, and when Alan woke in the morning he found her already up.

'I've got that address, Alan,' she said. 'Will you do something for me, when you're in the library?'

'Yes, if I can,' said Alan. What address did she mean, he thought drowsily.

'Will you look in the London telephone directory and see if there's a J. W. Hampton – James Walter Hampton – at this address?' She thrust the paper towards him.

'He's sure to have moved,' said Alan. 'But he might still live in London,' he conceded. 'Of course I'll look, Louise.'

'And write down the address, if you find him in another area?'

'Yes, my darling.'

'Oh Alan!' She cast herself upon him. 'It's so wonderful

having you here.' She was liking this new, full-time pairing.

They wouldn't have many chances like this, Alan thought; Daphne was so seldom away. But she'd go to see Pauline more when the baby was born, he thought, brightening; grandmothers did.

That afternoon, he returned with a short list of Hamptons neatly copied from the E–K volume of the telephone directory. There were three with the right initials, and one of these was in Putney. The address on Louise's birth certificate had been Putney, too, though different from this one.

'That's him!' she said. 'I know it is! I'm going to see him.'

'Better telephone first, to make sure,' Alan suggested. 'Or write. You could enclose a stamped addressed envelope; then there'd be an obligation on him to reply.'

'No. If I do that, he might put me off – say it wasn't convenient. But if I just turn up, he'll have to see me,' said Louise. 'I've got to do it, Alan.'

She was very quiet that evening, and for the first time, slow to respond to Alan's caresses.

In the morning, going to school with Tessa, she said, 'Darling, I'm going to London today, on business. I'll be back before you come home from school, but you've got your key if for any reason my train is late, so let yourself in and I'll soon be there.'

'But you'll meet me, Alan, won't you?' said Tessa.

'Sweetie, I'm going for an interview to a factory forty miles away,' said Alan. 'I won't be able to get here in time.'

He felt utter dismay. Louise had waited until now to tell him her plan, when Tessa's presence prevented him from marshalling argument.

'Don't worry, then, Mummy,' Tessa said staunchly. She felt under her coat; the key was there, round her neck, beneath her clothes.

'I will be back,' Louise insisted. 'There's a two-fifteen train – I'll catch that, at the latest, but sometimes they do run late, Tessa,' she warned.

'Couldn't you go next week?' Alan said. 'I'd go with you, then.'

'I must do it alone,' Louise said. 'And I must go while I've got my nerve.'

'I wish you wouldn't,' said Alan, and Tessa felt her skin prickle. His voice had sounded funny, not like Alan's kind voice at all, but almost cross. Her mother didn't reply. What had she meant about nerve?

'See you on Monday, Tessa,' said Alan, when she got out of the car. He would have to go straight home after his interview for Daphne was coming back that day. This morning he must make sure there were no clues about to point to his absence. He'd left the telephone off the hook in case any callers wondered about it being unanswered and he must replace the receiver besides sorting out the larder, where the bread was probably mouldy, and there would be today's milk and papers to take in. All this needed so much managing, without Louise suddenly taking it into her head to go sleuthing.

'Please don't go to London today, Louise,' he repeated when Tessa had gone into school. 'Can't I persuade you to wait?'

She shook her head.

'I must do it,' she said. 'I'll never be right until I know about him. It's holding me back, somehow.'

'But he may be at work,' Alan pointed out.

'Then I'll ask a neighbour where he works, and go and see him there,' Louise said. 'I can't go at the weekend, Alan, because of Tessa. There's no need for her to know what this is all about. Please will you take me to the station?'

'Have you got any money?'

'Yes. Fifteen pounds,' she said. 'That's plenty.'

Alan gave her the contents of his wallet and told her to take a taxi from Paddington.

'Don't try to cope with the bus or the tube today, Louise,' he said. 'That's asking too much of yourself. Now, promise.'

Louise promised. That was easy to do.

Alan knew that a few weeks ago she would not have been capable of undertaking a trip like this on her own. He tried to feel pleased that she had made so much progress as he stood on the station platform, watching the train disappear.

Louise had not waited to wave at the window. She settled into a corner seat, all her attention fixed on the day ahead.

She spent the journey gazing out of the train window reciting the Putney address in her head: 67 Widersedge Road. I'm going to see my father, she thought, and spun a fantasy in which they fell into one another's arms, twin souls reunited. But after a while she banished this dream. If they were twin souls, somehow or other he would have kept in contact with her.

At Paddington, Louise experienced a sudden and bad attack of the gremlins, the first for some time. Sitting on a bench on the station concourse, waiting for her thumping heart to slow and the dizziness to pass, she breathed deeply and thought that Alan's advice about taking a taxi was sound. She'd been to London so seldom and didn't know how to get around easily; already the crowds were daunting.

The taxi driver did not know Widersedge Road, but he had an idea where it was, a branch from another, bigger road. He drove slowly along a wide street, looking out from his cab at the names on the turnings. Louise peered out too. They both saw the sign, Widersedge Road, at the same moment.

'Drop me here, please, on the corner,' said Louise. 'I'll walk the rest of the way.'

'Sure, love?'

'Yes.' She got out and opened her bag. 'How much?'

She was trembling again when he drove off, but once more she breathed deeply, clenched her hands, and set off along the street which had rows of identical pebble-dashed semi-detached houses on either side. Here and there an owner had made some attempt at individuality, with latticed windows or a vivid front door. There were venetian blinds at some windows, and net curtains at many. Most of the small front gardens were neat. In some, daffodils were thrusting through the soil, a few already in bloom. One or two front lawns were shaggy with growth and some flower beds were full of weeds. It seemed a quiet area. Even numbers were on one side of the road, odd on the other. Louise was beginning her walk at the lower end of the register, on the even side, and as the numbers grew higher, her footsteps slowed.

She stopped on the farther pavement, a little way off from number 66 and looked over the road at number 67.

It was like most of the rest, duller than some, the unpainted pebble-dash a drab, sandy brown; the window frames and the door were black. There were faintly grubby net curtains shielding the occupants from an inquisitive gaze. Louise walked nearer. An almond tree, already breaking into bloom, grew near the fence; crocuses flowered beside the front path.

Louise glanced at her watch. It was just after eleven, quite a respectable time for an unheralded call, but she was surprised to see that it was so late; she must have spent some time at the station warding off her attack.

She crossed the road, opened the wooden gate, walked up the path, took a deep breath and rang the bell.

Her head spun as she stood there, and her heart began thumping again. An unreal feeling, as if she were dreaming and watching what was happening from some spot over-head, came over her.

The door opened and a small woman with grey hair and spectacles, wearing a much-washed blue jumper and a sagging brown tweed skirt, stood revealed.

'Yes?' she inquired.

Louise had not rehearsed what to say.

'Mr Hampton,' she said. 'Mr James Hampton. Does he live here?'

'Yes, he does. I'm Mrs Hampton,' said the woman briskly, and waited.

Mrs Hampton. Mrs Hampton was Freda. Mrs Hampton was Louise's mother.

She looked at this woman, shorter than herself, and saw that she was old. Her face was pouched round the mouth, and was lined. She looked much older than Louise's mother.

'What is it?' Mrs Hampton asked, as Louise stood staring at her. She sounded impatient.

'Is he in?' Louise asked, licking her dry lips. 'Mr Hampton?'

'Yes.' The woman glanced past Louise into the street. What she saw, or didn't see, seemed to reassure her. She opened the door a little more widely, but repeated, 'What is it?'

'Mr James Hampton, formerly of Farland Road?' Louise said, and felt her knees go weak as the woman looked startled.

'He did live there, yes,' she said shortly, and called into the house, 'Jim!' She glanced back at Louise, hostile now, and called again, 'Jim, there's someone to see you.'

Jim! That was her father! Louise was aware of no sound apart from the pounding inside her chest that was made by her frightened, desperate heart.

A man appeared at the back of the hall. He wore a v-necked Fair Isle pullover in shades of blue, and a green worsted tie. He was almost bald; what hair he had was sandy-coloured. He was wearing half-moon glasses over which his pale blue eyes looked at her in perplexity.

He could be the man in the photograph. It was impossible to be certain. He had not recognized her, but why should he? Louise did not recognize him.

'Yes?' he was saying, moving forward. 'You want something?'

Louise's pulse was steadying; the world had stopped swaying around her.

'I'm Louise,' she announced.

'Louise?' he repeated, puzzled. It seemed to mean nothing to him, but the woman stiffened and Louise sensed her tension.

'I think I'm your daughter,' she said.

'Oh – Louise,' he repeated, staring at her, blinking behind his glasses. 'Oh, Louise,' he said again.

It was Mrs Hampton who recovered first.

'You'd better come in,' she said. 'Now that you're here.'

She had found the right man, though he was gaping at her as if he still had not understood. Louise stepped into the narrow hall and Mrs Hampton closed the front door. There was some manoeuvring as they re-formed, James Hampton standing back to let Louise enter the sitting-room first.

The others trooped after her. It was a small room, and shabby, but snug. A gas fire was alight in the hearth; daffodils, arranged in a blue glass vase, stood on a modern oak chest of drawers of the kind that could be bought in any large furnishing store. There were a few books, mostly paperbacks, in a recess by the fireplace, and a newspaper, the *Daily Mail*, lay open on the sofa. Across the room an elaborate stereo system occupied most of one wall, with shelves full of records; this was the only touch of luxury in the room.

'Well, Louise,' said her father, and repeated, 'Well!'

'I thought you were dead,' Louise burst out. 'I only found out a few months ago that you might not be.'

'Oh!' said James Hampton. 'How strange!'

'Sit down,' said Betty Hampton. What did the girl want? Money? She was quite well dressed in a dark green skirt, matching dark tights, long boots, and a hip-length camel coat.

Betty Hampton had always feared this would happen one day, though as the years passed, the chance seemed less likely. She'd better make coffee, give them all time to collect themselves. The girl was quite pale and seemed nervous. Jim must have had a severe shock, hearing her say who she was like that. She suggested the coffee, aloud, and Jim signalled with his eyes that he did not want to be left alone with this stranger. He'd better not lose his head, whatever lay behind this extraordinary visit.

'Have you come far?' Betty asked, and Louise told her she had come from Berbridge by train to Paddington.

'Then you'd like a wash,' Betty stated. 'Come along, Louise. I'll put the kettle on while you're upstairs.'

She was bossy, Louise thought, as was Freda; but she was much softer-looking, and in a way pretty, still, though so old.

Louise went upstairs meekly.

There was worn lino patterned in a green marbled design on the bathroom floor. Two flannels, one blue and one pink, hung on a rack over the stained, yellowing bath. There were faded print curtains at the window. Two large turkish towels, their edges fraying, one blue and one pink, hung over a rail.

It was very clear that her father was not well off, Louise thought, washing her hands at the basin where soap scum lingered round the taps, and his wife was no great house-keeper. She dried her hands gingerly on a corner of the blue towel.

A door was ajar on the tiny landing. Louise paused at the top of the stairs and listened. Sounds came from below where, in the kitchen, her father's wife was making the coffee.

Louise pushed the door wider, far enough to let her look into the front bedroom of the small house. She saw a large, sagging double bed, covered with a pink candlewick spread. Across one corner of the room stood a kidney-shaped dressing-table adorned with pink skirts printed with dark red rosebuds, matching the sprigged curtains at the bow window through which now streamed the mid-morning sun. A shiny pink dressing-gown was draped over a chair; a pair of pink, fluffy mules lay on the floor, not neatly together but one in a corner and one on its side near the bed. The carpet was off-white, stained here and there. A scent hung in the air; musky, even sultry. To Louise it was a strange room, and the thought flew into her head that a prostitute's room might be like this. She withdrew quickly, ashamed of her prying.

At the hotel, her mother's room contained a narrow single bed covered with a spread patterned in sharp geometric designs in green on a brown background. The carpet was dark brown, and so were the curtains. The dressing table, like all the rest in the place, was modern light oak.

Louise went slowly down the steep stairs. The carpet, dark red, was threadbare.

'Sugar?' called Betty Hampton from the kitchen, hearing her.

'No, thank you,' said Louise at the kitchen door.

She prepared herself for a further great contrast, though you couldn't fairly compare a hotel kitchen, with its almost clinical cleanliness, with an ordinary family kitchen.

Betty's kitchen had red and white checked curtains at the

windows and a red formica-topped table in the centre, with four spoke-backed chairs round it. A scrubbed dresser with open shelves bearing a mixed collection of plates and dishes stood against one wall. There was a rack on the drainer containing the breakfast dishes, blue and white Cornish ware. A saucepan stood at the side of the sink and on a newspaper beside it there was a pile of sprout leaves. Betty had been preparing the vegetables for lunch when Louise arrived.

Three large cups and saucers of the same Cornish ware were ready on a plain wooden tray, and into them Betty poured fresh coffee which she had made in an earthenware jug. She added sugar to one and gave it a stir, then milk to them all. Some homemade shortbread was arranged on a plate. So he'd found another good cook, Louise thought, though this one was also, it seemed, a bit of a slut.

The coffee with sugar was for her father.

Suddenly Louise remembered a sandy-haired man with a soft moustache heaping sugar into a china cup.

'He had a moustache,' she said abruptly. 'My father.' He was cleanshaven now.

'Yes,' agreed Betty Hampton. 'He took it off long ago.'

She picked up the tray and led the way back to the sitting-room, where James Hampton had tidied his news-paper away and plumped up the sofa cushions. He looked at Louise in what she identified as a sheepish manner.

He's a weak man, she thought, with a sinking heart. Then, remembering the room upstairs with the sagging bed and the scent in the air, she glanced at his wife. Somewhat shocked at the direction her thoughts were taking, she found herself speculating about her father's life with this faded woman. What about her mother? How had that been? Questions that would never have occurred to Louise a few weeks ago now sprang into her mind: so much had Alan done for her.

She took the cup and saucer her father's wife was handing to her, and watched her father accept his coffee. His hands were large and square; they shook slightly.

'You've retired,' she stated.

'Yes – last year, at Christmas,' said Betty Hampton.

'You've just caught us, Louise. Next week would have been too late. We're moving away.'

'Oh,' said Louise. 'Are you? Where to?'

'To the coast,' said Betty Hampton. 'We've got a nice bungalow, newly built, a hundred yards from the sea.' She didn't say where it was. 'We both like the sea,' she added.

So did Freda.

'Have you always lived here?' Louise asked.

'Yes. Your father took out a mortgage straight away – all those years ago. It's paid off now and we've sold well. We're having new carpets and furnishings in the bungalow. It's quite an excitement.'

Her father had still scarcely uttered. There were the first faint signs of pigmentation on the backs of his hands, Louise saw.

'We couldn't move far, you see, because of your father's work,' Betty Hampton went on explaining. As she spoke, she cast a glance at her husband, reminding Louise of an anxious mother concerned for her child.

'What was your job?' Louise asked her father.

'Insurance,' said Betty. 'It was always that, after the air force, Louise.'

Insurance. His occupation on her birth certificate was given as clerk and Louise knew now, with sad certainty, that her father had risen no higher.

Her mother part-owned a thriving hotel.

Yet once he had been a pilot. In that old photograph, there were wings on his uniform tunic.

'Did you fly Spitfires?' she asked.

'No,' said her father, speaking at last. 'Lancaster bombers.'

'Oh,' said Louise. She looked at the plump, ageing man who did not want to meet her gaze. 'Where is Farland Road?' she asked. 'The address on my birth certificate?'

'It's just round the corner,' her father said. 'Your mother sold up and moved.'

'I don't remember it,' said Louise. 'Not at all. I don't remember a thing about those early days.'

'Your father gave your mother the house outright,' said Betty Hampton. 'He was paying it off for years.'

98

So that was how her mother had got her original capital! She'd used the money to good advantage. She was worth a great deal more now, in terms of cash, than her father. But what was he worth as a man?

'It seemed best to leave you alone, Louise,' he said now. 'Not upset you by making claims. If your mother had stayed nearby, maybe we'd have kept in touch – I don't know. But she whisked you away – disappeared with you. I didn't know where she'd gone.'

'She told me you were dead,' Louise reminded him.

'I expect she thought it was kinder to you – a clean break,' said Betty, who approved of what Freda had done.

'You don't look at all like your mother,' her father said. 'You're a pretty girl, Louise.' He looked pleased, saying this.

'You're married,' said Betty pleasantly, more relaxed now that it seemed this was purely a social call. She'd noticed Louise's ring.

I'm a widow, I'm lost, Louise screamed inside. I'm trying to pick up my life and find out who I am.

Aloud, she simply said, 'Yes.'

I've a daughter, Tessa, who's only six years old and who would like a kind grandfather somewhere in her life, she added inside her head, but instead of telling them any of this, she stood up. There was no place for her here; she was an intrusion and a reminder of things they preferred to forget.

'I must go now,' she said. 'I shouldn't have come.'

'Not at all, Louise. We're glad you did, aren't we, Jim?' said Betty, rising too. As she saw Louise to the door, she did not offer to give her their new address, and Louise did not ask for it. She knew she would never see them again. In her handbag were snaps of Tessa, both as a baby and more recently. There was no point in getting them out. These people had nothing to do with her.

Betty closed the front door before she had reached the gate. Louise did not see her father standing behind the net curtain, watching her leave.

She walked quickly down the road, a sick feeling in her stomach and her heart thumping again, but without any panic. This was no attack of the gremlins; this was rage.

Once round the corner, she stopped. Farland Road, they had said, was not far away. She might as well take a look at where she had lived as a child.

She asked a woman pushing a pram where it was.

12

The house was built of dull, brownish brick. Long windows under a gabled roof reflected the March sunlight, giving them a blank appearance. The front door was painted yellow.

It should be green, Louise thought: dark green. She stood by the gate of number 33 Farland Road and looked up at the tall, narrow, Edwardian house with the short flight of stone steps leading to the front door.

She opened the gate and walked up the path. There was a wide letter-box, made of brass and gleaming, set into the front door, and a heavy brass knocker. Louise climbed the steps and lifted the knocker.

It was easy to reach; there was no need to stand on her toes, she thought, and knew that, long ago, she had had to do that to announce she was there, outside.

A loud, single thud echoed through the house as she let the knocker fall. She heard sounds from within, and as the door opened she knew that there would be a seascape painting on the wall at the left, and a coat rack on the other side of the hall. Steep stairs would ascend at the rear.

The front door opened, and a blonde girl with an inquiring expression stood revealed. In a strong accent, she said, 'Yes? What is it, please?'

Louise looked past her.

The hall was painted white. Several small prints hung at the left; there was no coat rack on the other side but a large central heating radiator with a shelf above, on which some small porcelain figures were displayed. At the back of the hall, the stairs rose steeply to the upper floors. They were not covered with the green and brown carpet like jungle undergrowth which Louise expected but in plain apricot colour. The banisters were painted white, and more prints hung in groups on the walls.

'Yes, please?' the fair-haired girl was repeating.

Louise brought her gaze back to the smooth, youthful face.

'Louise Hampton,' she said. 'I'm looking for Louise Hampton. She lived here, once.'

'Is no Hampton here now,' said the girl earnestly. 'Is Mr Renton and Mrs Renton. Since some years.'

'It was some time ago,' Louise acknowledged. 'She was only a child – eight or nine years old.'

'Mrs Renton is out now. Is coming home this afternoon,' said the girl. 'You come back. She tells you then.'

A wail came from somewhere inside the house.

'Is the baby,' the girl said. 'You come again. You ask to Mrs Renton.'

Louise shook her head slowly.

'Never mind,' she told the au pair girl. 'It doesn't matter now. I think it's too late to find her,' and she turned and walked away, leaving the girl staring after her in bewilderment before the increasingly loud yells from her charge prevailed.

Her room had been on the top floor, Louise knew; the route upstairs was through the deep jungle growth, menaced by lions and tigers. She had a white chest of drawers and her clothes hung in a white-painted wardrobe. Her curtains were blue, with small daisies on them, and there was worn dark blue haircord on the floor.

Her parents' room was on the floor below: twin beds with a wide space between, and beige silky counterpanes. The curtains were beige too, and the carpet.

In the kitchen, her mother would be cooking the supper; savoury smells would greet her; there would be dripping toast for tea on cold days after school. Her father, when he came back from work, would kiss her, his soft moustache brushing her face, and would give her a toffee from a bag he kept in his overcoat pocket. Her mother mustn't know about the toffee, for sweets were bad for the teeth. Her father would slick down his thinning sandy hair with a brush, looking at himself in the glass to make sure he was neat. She remembered now that he never went into the kitchen to greet her mother; he'd go into the sitting-room where he'd read the paper, and Louise would do her homework at the table beside him. She didn't have much homework yet; she was rather young for a lot. Sometimes there wasn't any, but she'd pretend there was and would read or draw, because she liked being there with her father. Later, he'd read to her, or she'd sit on the floor with a book. They wouldn't talk much, but it was cosy. Sometimes he'd play records, rather softly, for her mother didn't like loud symphonies or choirs.

Louise seldom had a friend in to play, she recalled, though sometimes she went out to tea with other little girls. Her mother didn't encourage socializing; children around made a mess. Besides, Louise was to work hard and get to the grammar school.

Then one day the house was empty. There were no curtains, no furniture, no one inside, when she came home from school.

Louise almost screamed again, standing in the road, remembering that day.

She missed the 2.15 train back to Berbridge, and there wasn't another until an hour later.

Louise didn't know what happened to the time in the interval between leaving her father's house and reaching the station. She'd walked blindly round the streets, her head full of images from the past, coming back again to stand opposite 33 Farland Road while memory crowded upon her.

She'd stood there, screaming, eight years old. Then, from the next house, number 35, which now had white window paint and a blue front door, her mother had come stalking out to rebuke her over the fence dividing the paths.

Louise had been too hysterical to hear the sharp words, but her mother had marched down the one path, up the other, and caught hold of her roughly, shaking her, ordering her to be silent, finally slapping her, and at that Louise had ceased screaming.

They had gone into the neighbour's house, where tea was waiting, but Louise had eaten nothing nor drunk the milk the neighbour had poured into a tall glass with a wavy pattern on it. Louise could see the tea table now, with the milk, bread and butter and raspberry jam, a dundee cake.

A taxi had come and she and her mother had driven away, with some luggage. They'd gone to a railway station and got into a train. She'd asked where they were going and her mother had answered, 'You'll see in good time.'

Hours later, when it was quite dark, they'd left the train at a small, remote station, dimly lit. It seemed to be the middle of the night. Louise had slept for a while in the train. Then there'd been a ride in a car, for quite a long way, and at last they arrived at a large house which Louise couldn't see very well in the dark. She'd been put to bed in a small room with a sloping attic roof: her home for the next two years.

Much later, she'd asked where her father was. Now, so many years afterwards, Louise could remember that he hadn't been at home for some time before this terrifying incident, but she'd been given no explanation for his absence. It was at the hotel in Wales that her mother had said he was dead.

Louise walked blindly round the quiet residential streets of Putney, remembering. Never once did she have an attack of her gremlins, but she took no heed at all of where she was and it was a long time before she returned to the present.

She heard a clock strike two, and remembered her train.

It was hopeless to expect to catch it now, though she ran back to the High Street and found a taxi fairly quickly.

Tessa would be all right, she thought in the train. She'd been warned and she'd go straight home. She'd done it often enough before.

But always, before, Louise had been there when she came in; Tessa had never returned to find the flat empty. Now she would return, as Louise had done herself so many years ago, to find no one there.

It wasn't the same. She had a key and could get in, and the furniture – all their possessions – would be there. Louise tried to console herself, arms clutching each other across her body, as the train carried her back to Berbridge.

Mrs Cox, she thought: she's not often out so late. Tessa will go down to her if she's frightened.

It had not been a normal day.

Mrs Cox sat in her basement room watching the window and wondering what Louise and the man were doing. After the morning's departure with Tessa for school, they had not returned. He'd been there all night again – the third night running. Mrs Cox would have complained to the landlord if she hadn't had other plans.

Throughout the day, she waited and watched, only leaving the window to prepare her lunch and to visit the bathroom. Once, in the afternoon, she went out to see if the green car was parked outside, but it was not.

By the time Tessa was due back from school, she was certain there was no one in Louise's flat, but she knew they now went, most days, to the school together.

She was ready, though, in case this should be the chance she had been waiting for.

At twenty minutes to four the small pair of legs that she had seen skip lightly by, in company, that morning, moved slowly past the barred window, alone.

Mrs Cox felt a surge of excitement. She got out of her chair and moved closer, watching for the adult pairs, but no one else came, and Mrs Cox, after only a short pause for thought, went out to the kitchen to fetch the mug with the Peter Rabbit pattern upon it which Tessa always used when she came to the basement flat. Into its base she poured, straight from the bottle in the bathroom cupboard, a large measure of Mavis's chloral hydrate; then she crushed and added some of the white sleeping tablets. She took the mug back to the kitchen and added a generous amount of drinking chocolate powder and plenty of sugar, for she knew the chloral hydrate had a bitter flavour. The prepared Mars Bar was still in her bag and she took it out. It would be a nice treat for the child. She poured some milk into a pan and placed it ready on the gas stove. All was prepared.

There was enough chloral hydrate left for several strong doses, and more white tablets, too, if this wasn't enough, Mrs Cox thought. But Grace had never awakened after consuming the contents of her mother's blue capsules, all those years ago.

Her hand on the door that led from her living-room into the basement well, Mrs Cox paused and glanced round. Her eyes rested on the oak chest, in which was the mohair rug that would make a soft nest for a sleeping child until she could be disposed of.

Mrs Cox smiled to herself and opened the door. She climbed the steps that led out of the well and walked round to the twisting iron stairs.

Tessa felt quite forlorn when she found that her mother was not waiting for her outside the school. It was a long time, now, since she had walked home alone. She set off slowly; perhaps she would meet her mother on the way. Busy all day at school, she had not thought about the mysterious errand that had taken her mother to London; business, Mummy had said. She had said the train might, just possibly, be delayed, but as Tessa trudged on she began to fear that her mother had had one of the attacks that had once been so frequent. Her feet dragged as she walked through the recreation ground, going slowly, hoping her mother would be coming towards her or perhaps waiting by the swings.

She wasn't. There was only a mother with a pram and a very small toddler in the play area. Tessa put on speed as she crossed the football pitch, for sometimes there were bigger children there, boys who called out rude things when she went by alone, but there was no one there today.

She walked through the gates and along Shippham Avenue, hurrying past the holly bush on the corner because of the dragon, not stopping to see if he snorted with fire today. She turned into Oak Way, sure that her mother would be at home by now but fearful of finding her pale and trembling again. She walked slowly past Mrs Cox's basement windows and up the twisting stairs to the flat. Forgetting about the key round her neck, she rang the bell.

No one came.

Tessa felt a strange sensation in her chest, a panicky flutter. Then she remembered her key. She took off her red gloves and stuffed them into her pocket. She fished inside her clothes and found the key, pulled it out on its long tape and fitted it into the lock. She turned it and went inside.

The flat was so quiet. She knew at once that no one was there, though she called out, 'Mummy!' and then, more desperately, 'Mummy, Mummy!'

This had never happened before. Her mother may not have met her at school every day, but she had always been here, ready to hug her and welcome her home.

Tessa slipped off her satchel and hung it on the back of the hall chair. She went into the sitting-room. Her mother had plumped up the sofa cushions and straightened everything before they all went out that morning. In the kitchen, the breakfast dishes had been washed up and left in the rack to dry. It had been nice having Alan there for breakfast the last few mornings. If only he were here now, Tessa thought, she'd feel better.

Tears came into her eyes. She was frightened, but that was silly – she was a big girl now, nearly seven, and no longer a baby. Her mother would soon come from the train, in a taxi, probably, as they had done together after visiting Grandma in Cornwall. She'd want tea. Tessa would get it ready – have it waiting when Mummy arrived.

The doorbell rang.

Mummy? But Mummy would come in with her key.

Could it be one of those bad men her mother had said she must never talk to? But they didn't come to your house, did they? Mummy always put the chain up on the door at night, though, so perhaps they did. Tessa put the chain on before opening the door. She peered through the crack.

Mrs Cox stood outside.

'Mummy's not here,' said Tessa, and her lip trembled.

'I know,' said Mrs Cox, and her voice was strong as she felt triumph near. 'Open the door, Tessa, and let me in.'

Tessa fumbled with the chain, finding it difficult, now, to

undo, but she managed, and Mrs Cox stepped inside. Tessa felt better already.

'Mummy's in London,' she said. 'On business.'

'Ah,' said Mrs Cox. Was she, indeed? What sort of business? In one of those shady hotels with her fancy man, no doubt, she thought grimly, though they'd had no qualms about carrying on here in what had been, until lately, a respectable house. She knew just what to say to Tessa.

'You must be a brave little girl,' Mrs Cox said, peering down into Tessa's face.

Mrs Cox had long grey hairs on her upper lip, Tessa saw; she'd noticed them before. They weren't very nice. They twitched as she spoke. There were some on her chin, too.

'Mummy's had an accident – a bus knocked her down,' Mrs Cox said. 'She's in hospital in London. You're to stay with me until she gets better. I'll take you to see her soon. Come along with me now.'

The world spun around Tessa. She felt sick and giddy. Her heart thumped and her mouth went dry. She allowed Mrs Cox to take her hand.

Mrs Cox noticed the satchel on the chair. She picked it up and carried it down; it wouldn't do to leave that behind.

Tessa had felt quite hungry when school was over, but her appetite had gone by the time she was sitting at the table in Mrs Cox's back kitchen.

Mummy was hurt – run over by a bus and in hospital. Daddy had been in hospital too, after being hit by a lorry when out in his car on the way to work, and he had never come back.

Would Mummy be going to Jesus too?

'An ambulance came,' Mrs Cox said. Children liked stories. 'Its bell rang, and it came very fast. Men picked Mummy up and took her to the hospital and a clever doctor is making her better. She's broken her leg.'

Just a broken leg. Tony at school had broken his, falling out of a tree. He walked about now with a plaster on, and bare toes protruding.

'And a bump on the head,' Mrs Cox went on. 'So that she went to sleep and didn't know what was happening.'

Mrs Cox could picture it all as if it were true: the blue light flashing, the stretcher men stooping to pick up their burden.

'She said you were to be good and eat up your tea,' Mrs Cox embroidered.

'But you said she was asleep,' Tessa pointed out.

'She woke up just as the nurse was going to telephone,' Mrs Cox said. 'Now, here's some hot chocolate for you, Tessa, as a treat. Drink it up, like the good little girl I know you are, and there's a Mars Bar too.'

Tessa picked up the mug with the Peter Rabbit pattern. She sipped the chocolate. It didn't taste the same as the chocolate Mummy made for them both, but it was very sweet and she drank it up.

Afterwards, Mrs Cox made her sit in the big armchair she used herself. She had turned it so that the high back was towards the window, and she had already drawn the curtains. She gave Tessa a book to look at, and told her to eat her Mars Bar. They'd play a game soon, she said.

The book was a photograph album full of snapshots of children in funny old-fashioned clothes. There was a newspaper cutting in it, too, not pasted in, but loose. The paper was brown and creased. It was a picture of a child – a little girl. Writing above and beneath the picture told some sort of story, but Tessa, afraid and miserable as she tried to spell out the long words, didn't fully understand their message. MISS-ING CHILD, she mouthed to herself but she was thinking really of Mummy.

She nibbled the Mars Bar. Wasn't there going to be bread and butter for tea? It tasted funny – sort of bitter.

There was something not quite right about Mummy and what Mrs Cox had said happened, but Tessa couldn't think what it was. Poor Mummy; had she cried, Tessa wondered, and a tear slid out of her own eye at the thought. She wiped it away with the back of her hand.

She ate some more of her Mars Bar, slowly. It would be rude not to finish it, but she really didn't want it; it tasted horrid.

Mrs Cox was watching her. She smiled as Tessa took a small bite from the bar.

'We'll play that game soon,' she promised, and got up to go out of the room.

Tessa hid the rest of the Mars Bar down the side of the chair, wrapped in her hanky. She'd rescue it later, and flush it away down the lavatory; then Mrs Cox wouldn't know how ungrateful she'd been.

But she'd had a lot of the sedative in the hot chocolate and it soon took effect. Tessa's last, elusive thought as she drifted off was about the telephone. Mrs Cox hadn't got one, so how – ? But she slept before the question had fully formed in her mind.

Mrs Cox waited a while. She tapped a spoon on a cup but the child did not stir. She tapped louder. Still no response.

Tessa seemed very heavy for such a young child, though she was, as Mrs Cox knew, rather small for her age. She lifted her up. I'm not as young as I was that other time, she thought; but she'd always kept fit, walking a lot, and cleaning and polishing the flat every day.

She lowered Tessa into the chest on top of the folded rug, and covered her with a crochet blanket Mavis had made. Next she turned her big chair round to face the window again. She pulled back the curtains a little way, and she watched the gap. She could not rely on her ears to pick up the sound of their steps on the path.

They'd look very foolish, the two of them, standing there with the traces of lust still on their faces, Mrs Cox thought, when they heard that Tessa had not come home.

She didn't have long to wait, but only one pair of legs went past, running.

Soon they came back, palely lit by the glow from Mrs Cox's window, as Louise clattered down to the basement.

She rang the bell and banged the knocker, but Mrs Cox kept her waiting, moving slowly to open the door.

White-faced, Louise gasped, 'Is Tessa here, Mrs Cox? She's not in the flat – I thought you'd – '.Her voice trailed off as Mrs Cox slowly shook her head.

'I haven't seen her,' she said. 'She hasn't been home.'

13

'You're sure?' Louise said, clinging to the doorpost of the basement flat. 'You're sure you never saw her?'

'Quite sure,' Mrs Cox asserted, and added, 'I usually notice when she – or anyone from your flat – goes in and out.'

Her intended irony was wasted on Louise, who, gasping with shock and fear, raced back to search the flat in case Tessa could somehow be hiding there, and then ran round the garden, calling and calling, seeking her child among the shrubs and trees in the gathering dusk. She looked in the shed where Terence Henshaw kept his gardening tools. No one else was at home at 51 Oak Way, for their various places of work hadn't yet closed for the day, although Louise tried all their bells, just in case.

'I must tell the police at once,' Louise said to Mrs Cox, who had closed her own front door and come to the top of the steps during this search.

Somehow or other, in her planning, Mrs Cox had not foreseen this, but it had happened that other time; it had been a policeman who found Grace in the boat.

'You were late,' she rebuked Louise.

'I missed the train,' Louise said wearily. 'But Tessa's come home on her own dozens of times before.'

An accident, she was thinking; she's been run over, crossing the road.

'Your friend,' Mrs Cox remarked, emphasizing the noun. 'Where is he?'

Louise stared.

'Your gentleman friend,' Mrs Cox enlarged. 'He was with you in London.'

Louise was not interested in the activities of the other tenants of the house so she had not realized that her own movements, and those of any visitors, might be noted.

'No,' she said shortly. 'He wasn't. He had an appointment.'

He'll help now, though, she thought, thankfully, and in the next instant remembered that she did not know where he lived or how to get hold of him. Meanwhile, they were wasting time when Tessa might be in a hospital ward wondering why she did not come.

'Perhaps he met her from school?' Mrs Cox suggested slyly. If Louise did call the police, Mrs Cox would enjoy telling them how she had seen this man alone with the child so often.

'He couldn't, today,' said Louise. 'Will you wait in my flat, please, Mrs Cox, while I ring the police? Just in case she comes back meanwhile.'

Mrs Cox agreed, and since the Henshaws, who had the only telephone in the building, were not yet home, Louise ran down the road to the nearest box. It was in the shopping area, and was working, though Louise, using one so seldom, didn't realize how lucky this was as she dialled 999 and asked for the police.

The voice at the other end of the line, when the police answered, was calm; its owner spoke slowly – much too slowly for the impatient Louise. But she was assured a police officer would come to 51 Oak Way at once; she should return there immediately.

Before she did so, Louise thought, oh, if only Alan were here, as he usually was at this hour! He'd search the streets in his car. And Tessa would recognize the Escort, if she had somehow got lost. If only she could speak to him, he'd come at once, despite his wife, she was sure. With trembling hands Louise turned the pages of the telephone directory, but there were dozens of Parkers, and a lot had the initial A. She couldn't wait to try them, and anyway he wouldn't be home yet from his interview.

She ran back, as fast as she could, to the flat, for Tessa might have turned up by now.

But she hadn't.

Mrs Cox waited until a constable in his patrol car arrived; he was very prompt. She listened while Louise told him her story, and added her own – that she'd seen no sign of Tessa, whose return, either alone or in company, she usually noticed.

The constable treated it very seriously. In a way, Louise was relieved that he thought her right to call help so quickly; he said that if Tessa had been involved in an accident and taken to hospital, the police would have been told at once.

'The child often comes home from school alone, officer,' Mrs Cox said, her tone condemnatory.

'Oh yes?' said the constable. He had already asked about the child's father.

'You'd gone off with your gentleman friend, of course,' Mrs Cox said, to Louise. The police must be told about him.

'I told you, I went to London alone,' said Louise. She wished the old woman would go; her usefulness was over.

'Where did you go in London?' the constable asked.

'What does that matter? For God's sake, start looking for Tessa,' Louise cried. The fact that she'd been to hunt for her father had no relevance to Tessa's disappearance. 'It was a business trip,' she added.

'I'll just have a look round,' said the constable, moving to open a cupboard.

His search was soon over. He wrote down a description of Tessa and the clothes she was wearing, and he asked for a photograph. Louise, silently, took from her bag the one she had planned to show her father.

'If only you'd asked me to meet her at school,' Mrs Cox was saying. 'You know I'd have done it – you'd only to ask.'

'She's used to coming home alone,' Louise said faintly. 'If she comes through the recreation ground there are no roads to cross.' She looked at the constable. 'I haven't been very well,' she said. To explain that she had agoraphobia would sound so silly. 'Tessa's very sensible.'

But the most sensible child could be enticed with a sweet.

'I see,' said the officer, noting it down.

'Oh, please start looking for her,' begged Louise. 'We're wasting time.'

'We have to know where to start searching,' the constable said. 'Now, Mrs Cox, will you stay with Mrs

Waring?' He turned to Louise. 'Or have you another friend who would come?'

Only Alan, Louise thought.

'I'll be all right,' she said. She didn't want the old woman. 'You've been very kind, Mrs Cox. Thank you.'

Mrs Cox felt certain that she had established herself in the constable's eyes as a kindly old lady. She wanted, though, to get back to her flat and her prisoner.

'Er – Mrs Cox, you spoke of a friend? Mrs Waring's friend?' the constable said. He'd better pursue this line, to complete the picture. 'Who is that, Mrs Waring?' he asked.

Louise gave Alan's name and added that she did not know where he lived. He couldn't have seen Tessa since they both dropped her at school that morning, she said, for he'd had a business appointment across the county that afternoon.

'He's got an old green car,' Mrs Cox said. 'It's often outside, sometimes all night,' she added, with a knowing look at the constable, and recited its number. The police would soon trace the owner from that and he'd have some explaining to do.

Louise was too distraught to pay any attention to this revelation of Mrs Cox's interest in her affairs. The constable simply thought her a typically nosy old party.

'Friends of Tessa?' he suggested, writing down the registration number. 'Other children? Might she have gone home with some other child after school?'

But Tessa had no particular friends at school, and apart from an occasional birthday party, didn't go out to tea. The possibility, though, gave Louise hope; something like that, unlikely though it might be, could have happened.

'Grandparents?' the policeman was saying, still writing in his notebook.

'My mother lives in Cornwall,' Louise said.

'Maybe Tessa took it into her head to pay her a visit,' the constable said, throwing out what he knew was an unlikely lifeline. 'Children do funny things. She liked it there?'

'Well, yes,' Louise agreed. 'But she'd never do that. How could she get there?'

The officer decided not to say that Tessa might have thumbed a ride.

'Kids get themselves even on to aircraft,' he said. 'Older ones, of course, and usually boys.'

He and Mrs Cox left together. The officer said that someone would be in touch with Louise.

At the top of the basement steps Mrs Cox paused to watch the policeman hurry round the side of the house, back to his waiting car. They'd be busy now, with their radios out and their house-to-house inquiries, but her flat was safe from a search; without a warrant, they wouldn't come in, and she'd said she hadn't seen Tessa. When the local hue and cry had died down, she'd dispose of that little one.

The river, Mrs Cox thought. The river would be the place.

Daphne had intended to be home well before Alan that evening, but an accident on the motorway causing a long tailback delayed her, and his car – still that shabby Escort – was in the garage when she arrived. He was in the study, listening to a flute concerto and trying to finish the *Daily Telegraph* crossword, when he heard her Mini outside.

In the mail, when he returned to Cherry Cottage that morning after his magical days and nights with Louise, was a letter offering him the job with the firm making electronic games. What should he do about it? If he didn't take it, he might remain unemployed for months. He brooded, pouring milk he should have consumed in Daphne's absence down the sink to leave the sort of amount she would expect to find in the fridge when she came home, and he went on brooding all day. This afternoon's interview had been for a much more suitable post; could he play for time until he heard about that?

Daphne, when she arrived, was full of news about Pauline. She'd promised that they would provide the pram for their first grandchild.

'I'll go up afterwards – when she comes out of hospital. She'll need a hand for a week or two,' she said.

Alan's thoughts flew at once to Louise. He'd be able to

snatch another spell with her then. He longed to know how she had fared in London, but he would have to wait till Monday to find out, unless he could slip off the next day to see her. He wondered what plans Daphne had for the weekend.

Daphne was still telling him about foetal scans when the doorbell rang. A uniformed police officer stood on the step. He asked Alan, who opened the door, if he knew a Mrs Louise Waring of 51 Oak Way, Berbridge, and being told yes, said he had some inquiries to make.

Something had happened to Louise! Had she had a panic attack in London and perhaps been taken to hospital? Alan's heart plummeted. He whisked the policeman into his study as Daphne went into the kitchen to take something out of the freezer for dinner. She felt only mild curiosity about the policeman's call.

The constable noticed Daphne's suitcase, still in the hall.

'You've been away?' he asked.

'My wife's been in York, visiting our daughter,' said Alan.

He closed the study door firmly, but he was sick with apprehension; a whole new area of vulnerability opened up in his life now because of Louise.

'Oh God!' he exclaimed when he heard about Tessa. What agony Louise must be in, he thought, but he experienced a gut reaction of relief because she, herself, was safe.

The constable inquired about Alan's movements that day. He'd spent the last three nights with Mrs Waring at Berbridge, had he not?

Alan wondered briefly how the police had traced him, since he had never told Louise where he lived.

'Yes,' he agreed, and added, nervously, 'My wife – ' letting the sentence trail off.

'She was away. Quite, Mr Parker,' said the officer. Adopting a moral stance over marital misdemeanours was not his role unless a felony had been committed. So far there was simply a missing child in this case. No crime had yet been discovered.

'What's happened to Tessa?' Alan asked.

She had been seen leaving the school alone, and setting

115

off to walk home, said the constable. She had never arrived.

'But Louise – her mother – ? She'd gone to London,' said Alan.

'She missed the train,' said the policeman. 'And was back too late to meet the child.'

He went on to ask Alan again how he had spent the day.

Alan described dropping Tessa at school and taking Louise to the station. He hesitated. Then the door opened and Daphne came in, obviously wanting to know why the policeman had called.

'There's been an accident,' Alan said to her, and added, to the constable, 'I was at the office as usual.' He gave the time of his return home, and when asked for his employer's name and address, supplied those of Biggs and Cooper.

When the policeman had gone, he told Daphne he must go out at once.

'What's happened?' she asked. 'What sort of accident is it?'

'There's no time to explain now,' Alan said. He was already through the door as he spoke. 'I don't know when I'll be back,' he called, and rushed from the house.

She had never seen him move so fast. In seconds he shot down the drive in his car, scattering gravel on his precious lawn as he passed. Daphne followed him out to put her own car away, and was just going back into the house herself when Bea Pearce went past, giving her boxer dog his evening walk. She stopped when she saw Daphne and asked about Pauline. Daphne supplied the news and Bea went on, 'Is Alan all right? I see he's not here,' and she looked at the empty space in the garage.

'Of course he's all right,' she said. 'Why shouldn't he be?'

'Well, when I went past this morning, the milk was on the step and the paper still stuck in the door,' Bea said. She'd noticed it the previous two mornings too. Usually Alan had left for the office by the time she passed each day with her boxer dog on his routine walk.

'Maybe he overslept,' said Daphne, but she frowned. Alan's system was geared to wake at seven every morning and even at weekends he rarely slept longer.

'Oh well,' Bea shrugged, and walked on, but she felt curious about Alan's break with habit.

An hour later, Daphne was wondering whether to start her own meal or wait for Alan. She was hungry and tired after the long drive, and the casserole warming through in the oven smelled good. Just as she had decided to go ahead, the telephone rang. It was Emily Peters.

'Ah – got you – glad you're back,' said Emily. 'I rang last night to give Alan the message, so you'd hear as soon as possible, but I couldn't get hold of him. I tried several times. It's about the medal on Tuesday,' and she went on to talk about golf.

How odd that Alan hadn't answered, thought Daphne, replacing the receiver. The telephone must have been out of order, for Alan never went out at night.

14

Chief Superintendent Drummer, head of the Berbridge Division, directed the search for Tessa himself. The child had not been missed till late afternoon; darkness was falling and the early March nights were cold. It had begun to drizzle. A small child, out in bad weather, might die of exposure.

But where do you start to look for a missing child?

Having established, for certain, that Tessa really was lost and not either hiding or hidden at home, inquiries had to begin at the school, which by now was closed. But teachers were traced and questioned about possible friends, and the crossing patrol warden was asked if she had seen Tessa leaving the school. She remembered her clearly, walking off on her own in her navy duffle coat, her woollen cap and her red gloves, with her satchel. She knew Tessa as a child who, until lately, had often gone home alone.

'A nice, quiet little thing,' said the lollipop lady. 'Poor lamb.' She confirmed that for the past little while the child's mother and a man, with a shabby green car, had often met Tessa, and a good thing too, for she was too young to cross the main road alone and she often went back that way.

Not today, however: the lollipop lady was sure of that; she had noticed her setting off towards the recreation ground. She hadn't needed to cross the road.

Police officers went to the homes of parents of Tessa's classmates, to make sure she had not gone back with a friend and to ask if any of them had seen her after school or knew where she might be, but there was no news at all. A house-to-house inquiry began in the area, starting between the school and Oak Way, fanning out as nothing was learned. Police officers went to the recreation ground and hunted there; they looked in the groundsman's shed, and they searched the boats moored alongside the river, shining torches in at the windows, as all the cabins were securely locked.

If the child had fallen into the water, she wouldn't stand a chance; the river was full now after the winter's rain, black and fast-flowing, too rapid and too deep to drag. Her body, if that was her fate, would perhaps be washed up later downstream, or possibly a garment – her cap or a glove – might appear. There were no signs anywhere on the bank to indicate that she had been there, but the path was gravelled, and would show no footprints. There were rushes along a stretch of the river and the police officers looked among them, in case she lay there, but there was no trace of her.

Chief Superintendent Drummer arranged for a loud-speaker appeal round the local streets, asking if anyone had seen Tessa, but nobody came forward. The woman who had been in the recreation ground with her baby and toddler had been so engrossed with them both that she had not noticed Tessa's solitary, silent passage past. She did nothing when she heard the loudspeaker request; she had nothing to say.

Tessa had vanished as completely as if she had been whisked off by a magic carpet.

Had a stranger been waiting, parked in his car out of

sight of the school, watching for a child who might be enticed away? Or had Tessa wandered through the gate leading to the recreation ground to the towpath and fallen into the river?

Either fate was dreadful to think of, but she might survive the first if she were found soon. There had been no recent local reports of children being spoken to by anyone sounding suspicious. A known sexual offender in the area was questioned and could prove himself, this time, beyond suspicion.

Tessa had not been seen at either the railway station or the main bus terminus. Conductors who had been on the local buses during the afternoon were asked if they had seen her, but no one had.

Darkness had fallen. Tessa was lost.

Children sometimes found their way into empty buildings. Everywhere possible would be searched.

Later that night, Mrs Cox picked Tessa out of her coffin-like place of concealment. She carried her into the bedroom, turned down Mavis's bed, and laid the child between the cool, spotless sheets, taking off her zipped boots before tucking her feet in. She should not wake for many hours, if ever again, but if she did, she would soon be sent back to sleep. She looked so pretty and peaceful, preserved in her innocence, Mrs Cox thought as she gazed down at her.

Before going to bed herself, Mrs Cox dissolved more of Mavis's pills in a glass of orange juice, and added some chloral hydrate and baby sedative. She put the glass ready on her bedside table in case it should be needed later.

The excitement had tired her. Mrs Cox was soon asleep in her basement bedroom, with her blue bulb burning.

A woman police constable came to see Louise during the evening. She asked her again about Tessa. Where might she go? What was she interested in?

She learned, in more detail, how often Tessa had done shopping errands on her way home and how sensible she had always been. Would she talk to strangers?

'She talked to Alan,' Louise confessed. 'She made friends

with him before I did. That was how we met,' and she told the officer how it had happened.

'So where was he this afternoon? If he usually came to fetch her from school with you, why not today?' asked WPC Frost.

'He had a job interview,' said Louise. She explained why he had so much time to spare.

Before she left to go back to Berbridge Central Police Station, taking with her Tessa's pyjamas from under her pillow in case it was decided to use dogs in the search, WPC Frost went to the ground floor flat, where the Henshaws had now returned from work, and told them what had happened. Jean Henshaw went up at once to see Louise, and asked her to spend the night with them, but Louise wouldn't move in case Tessa returned.

Jean stayed with her, trying to reassure her that Tessa wouldn't go off with some sinister man in a car, but that if such a man approached her, she might be scared and run away. That was probably what had happened; she'd got lost, and, as it was raining now, would shelter somewhere till morning.

But both women knew that if any law-abiding citizen found a little girl wandering about, one old enough to give her name and address, they would either take her home themselves or get the police as soon as they could.

'I just know something awful's happened,' said Louise. 'There's no other explanation.'

Jean thought so too, but it wouldn't help Louise if she agreed aloud. She tried to think of safe adventures Tessa might have. She was warmly dressed, in her duffle coat and her boots, and could withstand a certain degree of cold. If she got very tired, she might curl up somewhere and sleep. She'd be found in the morning.

While Jean was there, Alan arrived. He had made record time from Lower Holtbury, the car clattering as he sped along the main road. He'd slowed down through the town; getting stopped for speeding now would help no one, though he certainly hoped the police weren't wasting time on motorists when there was a child lost somewhere in the cold, dark and rainy night.

Jean returned to her husband.

'He seems nice, this Alan,' she told him. 'A good bit older than Louise, though. I'm glad she's got someone.' She felt guilty, now, at not trying harder to be friendly towards Louise, but the girl had always seemed so withdrawn. Today, though, Louise had told Jean about her visit to London, and confessed to her attacks of what seemed to be agoraphobia.

'If only I'd stayed at home today,' Louise had said, 'Tessa wouldn't be lost.'

'If only – ' Jean repeated. 'What sad words they are.'

If only she and Terence had taken more trouble, Louise might not have sunk so low.

'We must help her now, whatever happens,' she declared.

'Yes,' agreed Terence, silently hoping that this Alan, whoever he was, would do what was required.

Back at Berbridge Central Police Station, WPC Frost reported her conversation with Louise and what had been said about Alan Parker and his movements. It wasn't long before a disparity was noticed between Louise's version of how he had spent his day, and the account he had given himself. Alan had said he was at Biggs and Cooper as usual; Louise had said he was out of work and had been for an interview during the afternoon.

Chief Superintendent Drummer ordered Alan Parker to be brought in at once to explain this discrepancy.

There had been time for Louise to tell Alan a little about her day, but she seemed to have pushed most of what had happened in London out of her mind, except for regretting that she'd gone at all.

'Nonsense, Louise,' Alan said, though he shared her feelings. If only he hadn't had that interview himself: he'd have gone with her to London, and it wouldn't have been such an ordeal. They wouldn't have missed the train. But you couldn't go on wishing time back.

He tried to console Louise and make sense of what she was saying about her father and the other house she had called at, the one in Farland Road.

'You mean you came back from school one day and found it quite empty? No furniture? Nothing?' He was aghast.

'That's right,' said Louise. 'I suppose my mother thought explanations were pointless. She'd made up her mind what to do.'

'But not meeting you at school – ' Alan said. 'To let you come back alone and find that – '

'I always came back from school alone,' said Louise. 'I remember that now. But it wasn't far; there were no roads to cross. And I was older, by then, than Tessa is now. Besides, things weren't so bad when I was a child. So many terrible things didn't happen to children then.'

Alan wasn't sure about that. He thought they were simply more widely known about now.

It was useless for him to go out searching for Tessa. The police had scoured the district already and every officer on patrol was aware that a child was missing. They were still hunting where they could, though it was dark. There were factory premises and other deserted places where possibly, stretching expectations, a child might somehow have strayed. Such cases had been known.

Alan was trying to think of these and similar comforting theories to offer Louise when a police officer came to the door and asked him to go with him, please, to the police station. Alan had easily been found, when the officer sent to collect him from Lower Holtbury had learned that he had gone out.

'Something to do with an accident,' Daphne had said, bewildered, at the door. 'You came before – at least, another policeman did. An older one,' she added, looking at the smooth young face beneath its flat cap. 'I wish I knew what it was all about, but he left without saying where he was going.'

The policeman didn't enlighten her. Alan's car was soon spotted outside 51 Oak Way, where HQ had suggested it should be sought on hearing the officer's report.

'It's impossible. How could she be here?' said Freda Hampton, when a police constable from Portrinnock called at the hotel to see if her granddaughter was there.

Indeed, there had not been enough time since she disappeared for Tessa to reach Cornwall, even if she had been transported directly from door to door.

'We have to make sure,' he said.

'How could she be lost?' Freda demanded. She was very busy; dinner would soon be served. What a moment for such a visit. 'She's playing some trick on her mother,' she said. 'Hiding somewhere.'

'I hope you're right, Mrs Hampton,' said the young officer. 'Well, you'll let us know if she does turn up, won't you?'

'Of course, of course. But she's six years old. She couldn't make such a journey alone, and without any money.'

'Children do strange things,' said the officer. 'Hide in lorries and so forth.'

'She's not a troublesome child, at all,' Freda said. 'Quite obedient, and quiet. I'm very surprised.'

When he had gone, she went on stirring the sauce, but had to beat it quite hard as some lumps had formed. Ruth came in while, frowning with concentration, she worked at it.

'What a terrible thing, Freda,' she said. 'Poor Louise. You'll go to her, of course.'

'Why ever should I do that?' Freda said instantly. 'It won't help Louise to find Tessa. It's her fault the child's missing. She must have been negligent.'

'Even after all these years you can still amaze me, Freda,' said Ruth. 'Don't you realize that Tessa – your granddaughter – may have been abducted by some pervert? She may never be found alive. What do you think Louise is going through at this moment?'

'It's no good being weak and sentimental, Ruth,' said Freda, pouring sauce over the braised steak for table four. 'Louise must manage.'

'Someone must go,' said Ruth.

'Well, you can't, if that's what you're thinking,' said Freda. 'You can't leave the bar. She'll have friends – neighbours.'

But Ruth was remembering how Louise had fled from

her friends after Roddy's death.

'I'm going,' she said. Through her mind ran what must happen if Tessa were to be found dead: the identification of the body; an inquest; things Louise had had to face before. 'Louise isn't at all tough,' she went on. 'And no one should have to cope on their own with this sort of thing.'

'She was always weak,' said Freda. 'Like her father.'

And what about him, Ruth almost asked. What about the lie you lived about that? But this was no time to rake up the past.

'I'll ring up Marjorie and see if she'll come and hold the fort while I'm gone,' Ruth said. Marjorie worked as a receptionist during the season. 'If she's at home, I'm sure she will when she hears what's happened.'

'But you mustn't tell her. We must keep it quiet,' said Freda.

'Good God, why? It will be in all the newspapers tomorrow,' cried Ruth.

'One should keep one's troubles to oneself,' Freda said. 'No one will know it's connected with us, if it is in the paper.'

'I don't understand you, Freda,' said Ruth, not for the first time in their acquaintance, though it wasn't quite true. 'But I'm wasting no more time now. I'm going to telephone Marjorie.'

In less than an hour, Ruth was in the brake on her way to Berbridge. Freda, when dinner was over, went up to the flat as usual. Ruth hadn't even stopped for a meal; Freda had cut some beef sandwiches for her and put up a flask of coffee, since she seemed set on what seemed to Freda a ridiculous journey. How tiresome of Louise not to be on the telephone; a telephone call would have done, as it had after Roddy's accident. Ruth had wanted to go to her then, but Roddy's mother had flown over from her home in Majorca and there was no need for anyone else, Freda had said. She'd gone to the funeral and that was enough.

Louise was as feckless as her father.

Freda had put on the television, but for once she was not held by the screen. After a while she got up and went to the desk. She opened the bottom drawer and felt about under the pile of old magazines.

Her wedding photograph had gone.

She searched through the magazines and the rest of the drawers, but it had disappeared.

Freda felt shocked. She hadn't looked in the drawer for years, but she'd known that it was there, her one reminder that once she had been pretty, desirable and desired.

Jim had been so persistent; he'd been handsome, too, tall and fair-haired in his air force blue. Girls were eager to marry then, in the war; they took chances in case there would be none later and she'd been envied. It had been easy at first, for he'd been away most of the time, but when the war ended he was always there, and seemed unable to adjust to civilian life. Later, there had been Louise too, and they'd both wanted from Freda something she could not give. In the end, Jim had gone looking for love at the office. That's what he'd called it, though to Freda it had an uglier name. He hadn't done well at work, taking a long time to find a job after he was demobilized and then being passed over for promotion.

It was strange, Louise asking about him last time she was down, after so long. Had she taken the photograph? She'd no business to poke and pry. She'd wanted to know where they had lived, but Freda had put all that behind her, though it was the house in Putney that had set her on the path to prosperity. Without the money from that she couldn't have bought her share of this hotel. But not another penny had she had from Jim over all the years. She doubted if he had made many.

Freda felt uneasy, knowing that Ruth was not in the house. She so seldom left the hotel – only for her annual trip to visit her aged mother in Scotland each winter. Freda hoped she would drive carefully; it was raining hard here, though what it was like further east she did not know.

Ruth had promised to telephone, whatever the news, in the morning.

It was time for bed. Freda closed the desk, switched off the television, turned out the lights and went out of the room. Later, in bed, she closed her eyes and folded her arms across her chest, waiting for sleep, which was usually prompt.

That night, in her narrow bed, Freda lay wakeful, while scenes from the past jostled and jumbled about in her mind.

15

Why on earth did the police want to talk to Alan? And why take him off? Why not talk to him here, if they must, Louise wondered. They couldn't imagine he'd had something to do with Tessa's disappearance. Those men who molested children – even to form the words in her mind made Louise shudder with dread – were perverted: monsters. A man as kind, gentle and tender as Alan had proved to be couldn't be one of them. And he loved Tessa; Louise knew he did; he loved them both.

It was the first time in her life that she had ever been sure of someone's love. Yet she knew very little about him – a fragment or two; that was all. As he hadn't been able to tell his wife about his lost job, Louise decided his marriage was not all that marvellous. It seemed to lack trust. But she trusted him.

Why had the police wanted to see him?

Into her mind began to seep the dreadful idea that they had found Tessa in circumstances so terrible that they would not tell her, and were going to get Alan to do it – even identify her. Louise remembered what had had to be done when Roddy died.

She wouldn't believe it. Tessa wasn't dead. Somehow or other, she'd lost herself; perhaps some old person had met her wandering about and had taken her to their house, and would bring her home in the morning – some old person who hadn't heard the broadcast on local radio which had gone out that evening, or the police loudspeaker.

Louise sat alone in her first floor flat while Tessa was,

indeed, the charge of an old person and slept below in the basement of 51 Oak Way, snoring a little.

In the ground floor flat the Henshaws, too, were in bed. They clung together, comforting each other with love because the world was a frightening place in which terrible things could happen even on your own doorstep and into which, even so, they planned one day to bring children of their own.

When the doorbell rang, long after midnight, Louise thought it must be Alan. She rushed to open the door, and when she found Ruth on the step, fell into her arms, weeping.

Ruth hadn't been to Berbridge before. She hadn't known where Oak Way was. But she'd seen the police about; their cars seemed to be everywhere and there were officers on foot all over the place. A constable in a car had guided her all the way, as soon as she'd asked for directions. So she knew there was no fresh news; Tessa was missing still.

Mrs Cox woke early the next morning, as usual, and went to the bathroom. Then she made tea, but because Tessa was in the bedroom, she took the tray into the living-room and set it down by her chair. While the tea brewed she went back to look at the child.

Tessa moaned in her sleep, stirring a little. Mrs Cox put an arm round her, raised her head and held to her lips the glass of orange juice, heavily laced with drugs, which she'd prepared the previous night.

'A nice little drink, Tessa,' she crooned. 'Come along.'

Tessa's mouth was dry and she sipped automatically, slowly swallowing all the liquid. Some sediment remained in the base of the glass. Mrs Cox laid her back in the bed, tucking her in, then returned to her tea, closing the living-room door. She lit the gas fire and pulled her chair up to it as she drank her tea. Soon, comfortably warm, she dozed off.

Tessa, however, was roused by the act of drinking the cold orange juice, sickly sweet with sugar which Mrs Cox had added. The irritant chloral hydrate, interacting with the antihistamine in the baby sedative, began to stir up her stomach. She stirred restlessly, and wispy thoughts fluttered about in her head. There was something bad about Mummy but she couldn't quite remember. Waves of sleep pulled at Tessa, dragging her back towards unconsciousness, but her physical discomforts pressed too; she felt a bit sick and she needed to spend a penny.

Tessa struggled to sit up. She saw that she was in a room that was lit by a dim, blue bulb, and knew she was in Mrs Cox's flat. She'd been in the bedroom before, when Mrs Cox had shown her photographs of more of her children. Why was she wearing her skirt and socks in bed, Tessa wondered, and then she remembered that Mummy was in hospital and she'd come to stay with Mrs Cox. It seemed odd that they hadn't packed her toothbrush and pyjamas, though.

She did feel so sick, and her mouth felt all funny. She hadn't cleaned her teeth before going to bed, and that was naughty. Had she even washed? She couldn't remember.

She heard Mrs Cox moving about, then the sound of the living-room door closing. Tessa lay still, trying to ignore the sick feeling, and the other one, which wouldn't go away. She felt frightened, but Mummy would want her to be good and sensible and give no trouble to kind Mrs Cox.

Perhaps the nasty feelings would go if she lay quietly and pretended inside her head that something nice was happening. What would be nice? To go back to Cornwall – to go down to Portrinnock and out in Dick's boat, perhaps, catching mackerel? She tried to imagine it, dozing a little as she walked, in imagination, along the cliff path.

In the end, though, the sick feeling grew stronger, and she retched. How dreadful if she were to be sick here, in the bed that had belonged to Mrs Cox's dear friend Mavis.

Tessa got out of bed, moving cautiously, and tiptoed to the door. She eased it open. The lobby light was on as she flitted across to the bathroom and closed the door silently behind her. She had often been there before, to wash her hands before drinking the milk and eating the biscuits or banana Mrs Cox had given her so many times.

In the bathroom, Tessa was neatly sick into the lavatory bowl, making no mess, and not enough noise to wake Mrs

Cox who now slumbered in the armchair in the other room. After that, she relieved her bladder, then washed her hands and face at the basin. The thought of her unbrushed teeth still worried Tessa and she looked about for a brush, but the medicine chest on the wall was too high for her to reach and even if there were a brush inside, it would be Mrs Cox's and you shouldn't use anyone else's.

She washed her mouth out with cold water, and dried her hands carefully on Mrs Cox's towel, folding it neatly afterwards.

The plumbing, in the basement flat, was all at the rear, away from the room where Mrs Cox slept, unaware of her guest's careful activities.

Tessa crept back to bed. Her legs felt all woolly and odd, and her head very heavy, and she knew it must still be night-time. Though part of her was wretched with misery, part of her, too, was determined to give no trouble. Tessa knew, already, that when things were bad, crying and making a fuss wasn't any help and only made people cross.

If she was good, in the morning they'd go to see Mummy. Meanwhile, she was dreadfully sleepy.

Tessa had vomited up most of the second cocktail of sedatives, but the first one had not yet worn off, and she was asleep again almost at once.

'You said you were at the office today, Mr Parker,' said Chief Superintendent Drummer, sitting opposite Alan at a small table in an interview room in Berbridge Central Police Station.

'Yes,' Alan agreed.

'Biggs and Cooper, at Stowburgh?'

'Yes,' Alan said again, but his heart sank. Somehow the police must have discovered that he had lied. They might even suspect him of being involved with Tessa's disappearance. God, he'd been stupid! 'It wasn't true,' he went on. 'I wasn't in Stowburgh today. I've lost my job, but my wife doesn't know and she was in the room when the constable asked me where I'd been.'

'I see,' said Drummer. He stared across the table at

Alan, eyes hard in his rugged face. He had a small scar on his cheek, Alan noticed irrelevantly.

'I'm sorry,' said Alan. 'I suppose I should have rung you, or something, to tell you – to explain. Not that it can affect what's happened to Tessa.'

Probably not, as it happened, thought Drummer, but he did not intend to let Alan lightly off the hook.

'Where were you this afternoon?' he asked.

Alan told him about his interview.

'So you didn't meet Tessa from school?' Drummer said.

'I wish to God I had,' said Alan. 'Then none of this would be happening. But there wasn't time.'

Drummer wanted to know the name of the firm and, as he gave it, Alan thought that any chance he might have had of getting the job would disappear if the police came round asking questions about him.

Drummer noted it down. It would have to be checked, although instinct told Drummer that Alan was telling the truth now. Poor bugger, he'd got himself into a right old tangle simply through not telling his wife he'd lost his job. However, Drummer wasn't ready to let him go yet. The child's mother had revealed what he had been doing; now Alan Parker could supply details of her visit to London.

'Where did Mrs Waring go today?' Drummer asked.

'To London – you know that,' Alan said impatiently. 'It's how Tessa came to get lost. What are you doing to find her? You're wasting time.'

'We're not, Mr Parker. We're proceeding with our search,' Drummer said. 'But there's not a lot we can do now, until morning.'

'Well, let me go, then,' Alan said. 'Her mother's alone. You can easily find me again if you want me – I'll be at her flat.'

He really cared for the girl, Drummer thought.

'Tell me what Mrs Waring was doing in London,' he said. 'Why did she go?'

'To look for her father,' said Alan. 'She thought he was dead and she's just learned that he isn't.'

'Did she find him?'

'Yes,' Alan said.

'Tell me about it,' Drummer invited.

Early on Saturday morning, Alan was allowed to leave the police station. He was driven back to Oak Way, where his car still sat in the road outside.

He had telephoned Daphne.

It was Chief Superintendent Drummer's idea.

'You're entitled to make one telephone call,' he said, and grinned. 'Those are your rights as a citizen being questioned. If you were a sixteen-year-old vandal you'd know that.' He paused. 'Most folk ring their solicitor – you don't need yours, not at this stage.'

'I wouldn't hurt Tessa, any more than I'd hurt her mother,' Alan said.

'I believe you,' Drummer said. 'But I advise you to ring you wife, Mr Parker. She's probably going spare, wondering what's up.'

She wouldn't be; she'd be fast asleep, Alan thought. But he telephoned, all the same.

'There's a child missing, Daphne,' he told her. 'A friend's daughter.'

'What? Which friend?'

Daphne had answered after the first ring, though she sounded sleepy and cross, as she might, if she'd just woken up.

'Er – the girl you saw with my car that day in Berbridge,' Alan said. That part, at least, was true.

'Your new secretary?'

'Her daughter disappeared on the way back from school yesterday,' Alan said.

'Oh – of course you must help her,' Daphne said at once. 'Why didn't you tell me this last night?'

'I didn't want to waste time,' Alan said. 'I must go now, Daphne. I don't know when I'll be back.'

He'd said that before, when he rushed from the house, Daphne thought.

'What about her husband?' she said, but he had rung off.

She frowned, replacing the receiver. Why hadn't he told her more about this girl, Stephanie's successor? She pulled the bedclothes round her shoulders; the heating had turned itself off and there was no large, warm body beside her. She wondered how old the missing child was. What a shock for the mother. Yet why was it Alan who had to help? It was puzzling, to say the least.

A most unfamiliar sensation filled Daphne for the briefest of uneasy moments; then she banished the small, jealous pang. Not Alan: oh, no, she needn't worry. He had a soft heart, and he had a responsibility towards the girl, as she worked for him. Perhaps he was helping the police comb the streets, she thought.

She soon fell asleep once more.

Alan rang the bell at the flat. She wouldn't be asleep, he was sure; how could she be, alone and with Tessa still lost?

A strange woman opened the door. She was tall and thin, with very dark hair, and wore glasses. She put her finger to her lips and beckoned him in.

He thought at first that she must be a plain-clothes policewoman, sent to keep Louise company, but surely there weren't enough officers to spare for such welfare work when the child was still missing?

'You're Alan?' the woman asked, and when he nodded, went on, 'I'm Ruth Graham, Louise's mother's partner. I came as soon as we heard what had happened. Come along in. Louise has told me about you.'

Ruth had been glad to hear of Alan's place in Louise's life, though as he was married she feared that further grief and distress lay ahead for her, but at the moment there was no time for that sort of speculation. She led the way into the sitting-room, where one lamp burned. She had been lying on the sofa; a rug was thrown back against the cushions. Alan was just thinking how odd it was that Ruth had come, not Louise's mother, when she continued.

'Louise is dozing,' she said. 'I persuaded her to lie down, though she wouldn't undress. I told her I couldn't try to get any sleep unless she did, so she took a pill.'

'Oh, good,' Alan said. 'She must be exhausted after such a day. How did you hear about it? On the radio?'

'No.' Ruth explained about the policeman's call. 'Of

course Tessa couldn't possibly be on her way to Portrin-nock,' she said. 'Though an older child might try such a trip, perhaps. I suppose the police must have some sort of routine they have to follow.'

'Yes,' agreed Alan, and added, with feeling, 'They have to explore every possibility, including grilling someone like me.'

'Is that what's been happening? Louise couldn't think why they took you away,' said Ruth.

There was no need to tell her about the deception he had practised upon the police. The chief superintendent had turned out to be a very decent bloke.

'I think they call it eliminating someone,' said Alan.

'You could do with a drink,' Ruth stated. She'd picked up a bottle of brandy and one of whisky from the hotel bar before leaving; Louise was unlikely to have anything stronger than sherry, if that, in her flat, and it might be needed, she'd thought.

Alan gratefully accepted a strong whisky. He had had nothing to eat for hours, and, while he finished the sand-wiches Freda had made for Ruth, they talked. He told her what he knew about Louise's experiences in London that day and her childhood trauma.

'Oh no!' Ruth exclaimed. 'How dreadful!'

'You didn't know that had happened?' asked Alan.

'No. I hadn't met Freda then,' Ruth said. 'Poor Louise. What a shock for a child!'

'Yes,' Alan said grimly. 'She's paid for it dearly, hasn't she? Do you know about the attacks she's been having? It seems rather like agoraphobia.'

'No – she didn't mention that,' said Ruth. 'Tell me.'

'It seems they began after she went to see her mother last autumn,' Alan said, and explained.

'Louise said you'd been very kind to her and given her back some confidence,' Ruth said slowly. 'She never had much.'

'According to what I've read, agoraphobia can be caused by shock – often two shocks, a forgotten one, possibly, and then a second one which reactivates the first,' Alan said. 'In this case, her husband's death could have been the trigger.'

'Louise was lucky to meet you,' Ruth said abruptly.

'I haven't done much,' Alan said. 'Just tried to encourage her. Everyone needs encouragement.'

They were still talking when Louise woke and came into the room.

Ruth took her place, then, in the bedroom, and left them together by the gas fire.

There was no news by morning.

The police were busy in Berbridge. Once again they searched the recreation ground and looked at the boats moored along the bank, opening their canopies to see if by any chance Tessa could have climbed aboard one, but none bore any sign of disturbance. The search moved on; shoppers were questioned; the loudspeaker car went past again; deserted buildings, warehouses and yards were examined.

People volunteered to help in the hunt; young fathers called at the police station; even youths not keen on contact with the police came forward.

But where could they usefully look for Tessa? She had, it seemed, vanished almost immediately after leaving school.

That morning, the young woman who had been amusing her toddler on the swings in the recreation ground was discovered during door-to-door questioning. She had been there from about 3.15 for perhaps half an hour, she said, but was preoccupied with her own children and had not seen Tessa.

Would she have noticed if Tessa had turned across the recreation ground in the direction of the river?

The mother thought that was much more likely, for to do so Tessa would have passed directly in front of the swings on the way to the gate that led to the towpath. She thought she recognized Tessa from the photograph she was shown, for she was often in the recreation ground during the afternoon and had sometimes seen a solitary little girl walking past.

It began to look more and more as if someone in a car had whisked her away. She could be miles from Berbridge by now: in a ditch somewhere; buried in a copse. Every police force in the country knew, by telex, about her. Chief Superintendent Drummer had begun to fear that no more would be heard of her until a small body was found, quite by chance, some day, but his men went doggedly on with routine; by dusk on Saturday the area around the school had been toothcombed, and the whole town was aware that a child had been lost from within its bounds.

The search, of necessity, had widened its radius and moved away from the district where Tessa had lived.

It was quiet in the area around 51 Oak Way and its neighbouring residential streets, and that afternoon, because it was raining, there was no football played in the recreation ground.

Mrs Cox spent all day in the flat, sitting quietly in her chair. Now and then she looked at her prisoner, who still lay in bed, asleep, fair hair in its two small bunches lying on Mavis's pillow.

Mrs Cox had soup and cheese for lunch, and afterwards looked at her newspaper cuttings. Tessa was really very like Grace.

Mrs Cox had agreed to baby-sit that evening for the Bradleys in Shippham Avenue. It was only just round the corner, yet Mr Bradley always fetched her and took her home. Such good little children, the two little Bradleys were, guaranteed to sleep soundly all night. One was a girl, and fair; what would she be like when she started school, and how would life be for her then, wondered Mrs Cox. Would her mother be out meeting men, with Mr Bradley, unaware, in his office all day?

Mrs Cox sat in her chair turning the pages of the cuttings album, and the years fell away until, in her mind, there was confusion as to which child now lay in the bedroom. Some of the time she knew it was Tessa, whose mother had gone to London, but now and then she felt it was Grace from so long ago. She sometimes did muddle the names of her charges with those who had gone before.

16

Alan had not returned by the morning.

Daphne, at breakfast, glanced at the paper and saw a paragraph in it about the missing child, Tessa Waring, of Oak Way, Berbridge. There was a photograph, rather blurred in reproduction. The mother, Louise Waring, a widow, worked at home as a typist, said the report.

Daphne stared at it. First she took in the fact that Louise Waring was a widow; then she absorbed the description of her as working at home.

It must be a mistake. Papers often got things wrong. She hadn't been Alan's secretary for very long.

More disquieting thoughts came to Daphne. Bea had said the paper was in the door and the milk on the step when she came past with her dog while Daphne was away. Bea went by at a quarter to nine every day; you could set your watch by her, and whilst Alan might forget about the milk, he always looked at the paper over breakfast.

Physical activity was the best cure for worry, Daphne knew, so she got out the Hoover and vacuumed the house with vigour, though it was perfectly clean. She made some scones for the freezer, and a fruit cake with wholemeal flour. Then it was time for lunch and Alan had still not returned.

Surely he would be home soon?

Daphne took her lunch into the sitting-room and turned the television on to watch the sports programme. If she couldn't be active herself, at least she could look at others exercising themselves. Time passed, and Alan still did not return; nor did he telephone again.

Daphne went into his study later. There were some books on his desk, library books; she saw that they were about shock and psychological problems; rather morbid, she thought, but connected, no doubt, with that agoraphobic friend of his. In an absent-minded way, she opened a drawer of his desk. His sketch-pad was in there, and idly she glanced at it. She saw some rough drawings of a little girl in a duffle coat and ankle boots. She had a thin, rather peaky face and was, Daphne knew, the child in the newspaper photographs.

There were sketches of a woman, too: a young woman with large eyes, who resembled the child, the woman whom Daphne had seen near Alan's car in Berbridge that day. Daphne recognized her at once.

Late in the afternoon, Mrs Cox went to look at her captive. Soon she must prepare for her baby-sitting appointment and during the evening she would dispose of her small victim.

She had best prepare her now for what must be done.

Mrs Cox fetched Tessa's coat, which the child had placed, with her wool cap, neatly over the back of an upright chair in the living-room. She pulled back the bedclothes and began to insert one of Tessa's arms into the sleeve.

The child stirred, blinked, and drowsily peered at the old woman.

'Mummy – Mummy – ' she murmured.

She shouldn't have woken. Mrs Cox frowned. Of course, she was bigger than Grace had been, all those years ago.

'Mummy's in hospital. We're going to see her,' she said. 'Now put on your coat, like a good little girl.'

Tessa tried to wake up, but she couldn't, properly. Mrs Cox got her into her coat, fastening one toggle, and pulled on the red woollen cap. She put Tessa's boots on her feet, zipping them up, and placed newspaper under them to protect Mavis's bed. Tessa moaned a little.

'Lie still,' Mrs Cox ordered. 'I'll fetch you a nice warm drink, and a biscuit.'

Children always obeyed Mrs Cox's commands, and Tessa did now. Besides, she was dreadfully sleepy and didn't feel a bit like getting up. It seemed to be night-time still, for the curtains were drawn and the light was on. She lay back in bed, obediently, but she felt very worried about a number of things which she couldn't define. There was some big, bad, black worry, almost too bad to bear, she knew. She was trying to think what it was when Mrs Cox came back with two plain biscuits, and a mug of hot chocolate, normally one of Tessa's favourite drinks, but she didn't feel at all like drinking it now.

Mrs Cox propped her up in the bed, put a towel over the sheet against spills, and sat there, coaxing her to eat the biscuit and drink the hot, sweet chocolate. Tessa slowly munched and sipped; it was such an effort to eat. She still felt so sleepy. Mrs Cox held the mug to her lips, coaxing, encouraging, and down went the chocolate, containing more chloral hydrate, baby-sedative, and crushed nitra-zepam tablets.

Still propped against the pillows, Tessa heard Mrs Cox talking.

'I'll tell you a story,' she said. 'Shut your eyes.'

But they were going to see Mummy! Tessa tried to protest, but her voice wouldn't work, and her eyes wouldn't stay open though she tried so hard to make them. She heard Mrs Cox speaking and tried to pay attention. She was talking about a little girl with a naughty mummy, who left her to play alone by the river. The mummy liked shopping and buying extravagant things, and new clothes, and big dinners, and meeting her friend with his boat, like your mummy meets her friend with his car, Mrs Cox said, but Tessa was hardly aware of her words. Men and ladies were often wicked, Mrs Cox said. They played rude games and neglected their children. Tessa didn't know what that long word meant. Mrs Cox's voice droned on, monotonously, describing a house by the river and the good, kind nanny who wanted to keep the little girl – Grace was her name – from harm. Nanny and Grace played hide-and-seek, and one day Nanny showed Grace a good place to hide, in the boat that belonged to her mother, which lived in a shed like a garage beside the river. Grace went to sleep there, Mrs Cox said, and slept happily ever after and her mother was never naughty again.

Tessa's eyelids were closed.

'Go to sleep, Grace,' Mrs Cox said, but Tessa was already past hearing.

Mrs Cox assembled what she would need for the evening: her folding umbrella, a torch – Mavis had had a large one, and Mrs Cox always kept it in working order. She put them into her big black holdall, with her knitting.

Then she sat down in the sitting-room to wait for Mr Bradley to come. She heard the two girls from the top floor go past, heels clacking on the path; dates, she supposed, since it was Saturday. That was good. The Henshaws had gone out too; she'd heard busy steps above and a door bang; they usually did go out on Saturday nights. As for Louise Waring, she was upstairs, no doubt, with her fancy man. Mrs Cox had been too absorbed by thoughts of the past to watch for steps in and out of the flat today, but he was sure to be there.

For the rest of her life, Mrs Cox thought grimly, Louise would bear the punishing knowledge that during her daughter's last hours, she had been behaving immorally. She would go the same way as Grace's mother in the end, Mrs Cox felt sure, and a good thing too.

Before leaving with Mr Bradley, she turned all the lights out in the basement flat.

They met no one, driving round the corner to the Bradleys' house in Shippham Avenue. Mrs Cox peered out at the rainy evening. People wouldn't be walking their dogs in this downpour; they'd push them outside their doors and whistle them back, she thought. This was a quiet district anyway; even along Oak Way there was seldom much traffic except when the residents were going to work or returning. Soon, all those going out for their Saturday evening's entertainment would have left; there would be few witnesses to notice one old woman out in the rain.

It was a pity about the rain; it would make her task harder. But it would hold up the police too.

Mrs Cox had listened to the local radio which had reported the hunt for the missing child; she knew the search had moved on from the immediate area.

'What a terrible thing about that poor little girl,' Mrs

Bradley said when Mrs Cox arrived. She was so upset that she had wanted to cancel their evening out, but her husband had pointed out that their own children would be perfectly safe in bed, with admirable Mrs Cox, a former nanny, in charge, so what was there to fear? 'And she lived in your house, you knew her, of course?' Mrs Bradley went on.

'Oh yes,' Mrs Cox answered. 'A nice little girl.'

They sighed over the evil ways of the world as Mrs Cox took off her coat and hung it behind the kitchen door. Then the Bradleys departed, leaving, as always on such occasions, a delicious casserole dish in the oven, and a glass of red wine on the nicely laid tray.

Mrs Cox looked at the telephone number they had left; nervous Mrs Bradley always did this and Mrs Cox approved. Mrs Bradley was still a conscientious mother, though who was to say that would last. It was not a local number. Mr Bradley had said that the host was a business friend; Mrs Cox was sure they would not turn back.

The two children, unlike the Duncan baby next door, were dependable sleepers. Mrs Cox took the telephone off the hook so that if Mrs Bradley, or, indeed, anyone else, were to telephone, it would seem that the line was out of order.

Mrs Duncan had asked her to sit in this evening, too; the Duncans and the Bradleys were Mrs Cox's two most regular employers, and this time the Bradleys had asked her first. She preferred going to their house, given the choice; Mrs Bradley took more trouble with the dinner she left and the children were docile.

But the Duncans, tonight, would have had to find someone else: that schoolgirl they sometimes employed, no doubt. She would have the television on loud, or even her boyfriend there to keep her company. The baby was certain to wake up, and then the girl would bring him down and play with him instead of settling him firmly back into bed. Mrs Cox had heard Mrs Duncan describe what had happened before. At all events, the schoolgirl would be busy and occupied, and wouldn't hear if Mrs Cox made any noise as she wheeled away the large pram kept in the Duncans' garage. It was all working out so well. Even the weather, tiresome though it was, would keep away any nosy newspaper reporters who might want to talk to Louise; there had been a few round during the day and one had rung Mrs Cox's bell. She'd soon given him short shrift. They were ghouls.

She'd have to be quick.

Mrs Cox put on her coat and hat and picked up her zipped holdall. She let herself out of the back door and locked it, putting the key in her pocket. Then she walked round to the Duncans' house. She did not need her torch, as the street lamp outside cast enough light for her to find her way to the garage.

The doors were not locked. This had been her one worry. Mr Bradley always locked his, but the Duncans were less particular.

Inside the garage, stacked by the wall, was a pile of logs. The Duncans had only one car, and used the space in their garage for garden equipment and clutter. The Bradleys each had a car, and a shed in the garden.

Mrs Cox put a few logs in the pram. If anyone looked in it, she would say she had been given the logs and was taking them home. She set off down the road, round the corner and into Oak Way, where she pushed the pram through the gate of number 49 and hid it behind a large bush.

There was no one in sight as she entered her own gate, next door.

Tessa was heavy. Mrs Cox had a struggle to carry her up the basement stairs. It wasn't far to the gate, however, and again, as she peered cautiously out, she could see no one about. The houses on the other side of Oak Way, well set back from the road as they were, were dark, the curtains drawn across windows in occupied rooms. The rain poured down as, moving as fast as she could, Mrs Cox took her inert burden to the next garden. She had to wedge the pram against the brick wall of 49 Oak Way's boundary to prevent it from tipping as she placed Tessa inside. The child was far too long for the pram, and Mrs Cox propped her up under the hood, which was raised against the rain. She replaced the logs under the hood of the pram, where they masked Tessa, and put her holdall beside Tessa's head. Then she clipped on the pram cover.

Tessa's weight made the pram top-heavy. Mrs Cox leaned on the handle to prevent it from tipping up as she pushed it back along the road, turned into Shippham Avenue, went past the Duncans' house and the Bradleys', and entered the recreation ground, safe now from observation because there was no danger of anyone else being here on a rainy night, though in summer the place was full of teenagers up to no good in the dark.

Pushing the heavy pram over the sodden ground towards the river was hard work, and Mrs Cox needed both hands for her task. During her journey with the empty pram, she had been able to hold her umbrella above her head. The rain, however, was easing.

An hour after leaving the Bradleys' house, Mrs Cox was back there again, the pram restored to the Duncans' garage and the logs to their heap. She felt very tired, but also elated; it was done.

There was no sound from the sleeping children upstairs.

The casserole, still in the oven, smelled most enticing. Mrs Cox gulped the wine and searched for the bottle. There were often half-full wine bottles in the Bradleys' sideboard; she had topped up her glass before now.

Seeing brandy there, she took a small tot of that, and followed it up with more wine. Her coat and hat, hung by the boiler, were dry by the time the Bradleys came home and her wet umbrella was furled up inside her holdall. She was peacefully knitting when they entered the room.

17

Louise had known bad times before, but never in her life had there been a day like Saturday, stretching interminably ahead, hour after hour, each one seeming as long as a week.

They talked, in the flat. Ruth and Alan persuaded her to tell them in detail about her day in London and the meeting with her father. She spoke in jerky snatches, tracking back to Tessa every few minutes with new theories about what might have happened, but gradually she revealed the whole bleak tale. Ruth, since Alan had told her the bare outline, had been trying to think of some excuse for Freda's conduct.

'She must have meant to meet you as you came up the path,' she suggested. 'Perhaps you were one or two minutes early.'

'She never explained anything – then, or later,' Louise said.

'She doesn't find talking easy,' Ruth said. 'She must have been very badly hurt, Louise, at what happened – your father leaving her – so badly hurt that she couldn't bear to mention it – even think of it – ever again. And when you were a child, children were expected to do what they were told without question or explanation. All the same, it was a shocking experience for you.'

And Louise was so vulnerable, Ruth thought. Look at her now, with this dreadful time to get through and perhaps, at the end of it, desperate tragedy. During the morning Alan went out to buy food, since at least he and Ruth must eat even if Louise couldn't; he bought some papers, too, and they saw the reports of Tessa's disappearance in the home news pages. There was her photograph. It seemed quite unreal that this was their Tessa, thus described. The police were about, he said; he'd seen officers on foot, and patrols in cars, in the busier streets. They'd searched the recreation ground again, in daylight, and were asking in shops if anyone had seen Tessa the previous day.

But it was raining now. If she were alive, she was probably out in the open somewhere, lying unconscious.

Ruth started to do the *Telegraph* crossword, reading the clues aloud; anything to try to get through the time. Now and then she thought of an answer; so did Alan, at random. Louise wouldn't leave the flat, not even to drive about the neighbourhood, though she asked Alan to go in the afternoon, in case he might see Tessa somewhere; she would know his car, she said. If she left the flat, Tessa just might come back, and though Ruth would be there, that wouldn't do; it had to be her mother who was at home, waiting, when she was found.

In Putney, a woman officer from the Metropolitan Police called on Louise's father, whose name and address had been obtained from Alan.

'Your daughter visited you yesterday,' she stated, and James Hampton agreed that she had.

'What's happened?' he asked. 'Why do you ask? Is she in some sort of trouble?'

She'd been on his mind since she left; odd to think that the thin, wan young woman had been the small girl who had curled on his lap to be read to so many years ago. At first, when he left home, he'd often thought of her, but over the years he had learned to forget her, though sometimes, on her birthday, he remembered. Her mother, he knew, would take good care of her and see that she lacked for nothing. Louise had seemed anxious and edgy, yesterday, but, as Betty had said when she'd gone, she was adult and married and shouldn't need – she meant, expect – anything from him after so long.

'Have you not read the papers, Mr Hampton?' the policewoman asked.

'What papers? Is something wrong?' James's heart took a dive in his chest; he was going to be asked to take action, a thing he had seldom done since his flights in his bomber except for the one positive step of abandoning Freda. Surely Louise hadn't broken the law? 'Has there been an accident?'

'Not to your daughter, Mr Hampton. Your grand-daughter, Tessa. She's missing,' the officer said. 'Disappeared on her way back from school.'

'My granddaughter?' James gaped, then tried to hide his amazement while the officer asked about Louise's visit and took down a statement. James Hampton said Louise had asked about the house they had lived in when she was small and that he had told her it was not far away. The policewoman did not seem surprised when he said that he had not seen Louise since then. She asked for the other address.

After leaving the Hamptons, the policewoman reported in and received instructions to go round to Farland Road. There, she saw the au pair girl, who confirmed that a woman had called and said she was seeking a child named Louise Hampton, aged eight or nine, who'd once lived there. Her employer, out at the time, had no knowledge of any Hamptons when the girl asked her. Mrs Renton, at home this morning, confirmed this, and she and the policewoman decided that the au pair girl, with her imperfect English, must somehow have misunderstood what Louise had said.

Mrs Renton knew of the missing child and expressed concern; the visitor yesterday had seemed distressed, the au pair girl had said.

The policewoman went away. Perhaps the mother hadn't missed her train at all, but had met her own child, somehow attacked her, and then reported her missing. If she was having a breakdown, it could have happened; such things did. She went back to report.

'Louise has a child,' James Hampton said to his wife. 'Poor little thing – what can have happened?'

Betty Hampton thought it weird that Louise hadn't mentioned the child, nor the fact of her husband's death, which they'd learned from the policewoman. She must be a very strange girl, she decided, and hoped James would not want to make contact with her as a result of this business; it wouldn't do his blood pressure any good at all.

They'd been going to pack china today, ready for Monday when the van came for their move. She couldn't bear it if now, after all this time, something upset their plans.

'I expect she'll turn up,' she said.

First thing on Saturday morning, Terence Henshaw had gone to offer his help in the search for Tessa. While he was out, Sandra and Jenny from the top floor came downstairs to ask Jean if there was any news.

'It's so dreadful,' said Sandra. 'If only there was some way to help Louise.'

'We could feed them,' said Jean. 'She's got people with her – some friend of her mother's and her boyfriend.'

'I didn't know she had a boyfriend,' said Jenny. 'Is he nice?'

'Seems all right. Old enough to be her father, though,' said Jean.

'What were you thinking of?' asked Sandra. She and Jenny both had dates that night and it seemed a pity to cancel them, though they must, of course, if necessary.

'Tomorrow lunch, I thought,' said Jean. 'Most people like a roast on Sunday, don't they? I shouldn't think any of them feel much like cooking.'

'Good idea,' said Jenny. 'We'll help, won't we, Sandra?'

It was agreed, and they discussed plans over coffee.

'I've hardly spoken to Louise,' Jenny said. 'She's awfully quiet – never seems to want to stop for a natter.'

'Tessa's a sensible little girl, though, isn't she?' said Sandra. 'I've often seen her going off to school on her own, when I've been dashing to work, late as usual.'

'Yes, she is,' said Jean. 'But what does a kid that age know, after all? Tell her some sort of tale and she'd believe it.' She stirred her coffee. 'We've asked Louise round in the evening several times, but she'd never come because of leaving Tessa.'

'The old girl in the basement would sit in, wouldn't she?' Sandra said. 'She goes baby-sitting, I know.'

'I don't suppose Louise can afford sitters,' Jean said.

'She doesn't go out to work any more, does she?' asked Jenny.

'She does typing at home,' Jean said. 'It's better, I expect, with Tessa. She can work at night, and while Tessa's at school.'

But all three knew it wouldn't be as well paid as a job in an office, unless Louise did an immense amount of work. No overheads, though, beyond her machine, they agreed, and no need to worry about clothes for the office; but lonely.

They enjoyed their talk; it was strange, they thought,

that it took trouble to bring them together. The girls and the Henshaws had never done more than exchange a few words if they met in the hall.

Sandra and Jenny went shopping together that afternoon to buy things for the puddings they were going to make. Sandra bought a skirt, too; and Jenny a pair of shoes. Before they went out, Jenny whipped up an instant cake and took it down for Louise. The man opened the door and accepted it, thanking her gravely.

He did look nice, though his hair was ever so grey.

Ruth had telephoned Freda Hampton on Saturday morning, using the Henshaws' telephone. Freda was short with her, telling her she should return – that she couldn't stay with Louise indefinitely.

No, she couldn't, Ruth knew, and Alan was with her. She saw that he really cared about Louise, and about Tessa, too. If there was no news by Sunday evening, and if Alan could stay with Louise, she would come home then, Ruth told Freda.

For by then, hope of finding Tessa alive must be small; and no more might be known for weeks, if ever.

Freda sought about in her mind for a message to send to her daughter.

'Tell Louise – er – ' she said, and paused. The word 'love' was one she never used, and she could not frame any sort of affectionate message.

Ruth waited. She would not help.

'Tell her,' Freda said again, and then, with a burst, 'tell her not to stop hoping.'

Ruth passed on the exact message. It was good advice.

She felt very tired, and went to bed early on Saturday night, in Tessa's bed. Someone must try to be rested, for dreadful news might have to be faced. Later, Alan coaxed Louise into bed, and lay there beside her, holding her gently, not talking, till at last, because he was there, she dozed. He lay awake for a long time himself.

Down below in the basement flat Mrs Cox, exhausted, all her muscles aching, lay at peace in her bed, thinking of how she had carried out her mission and smiling in the darkness. Once or twice, she laughed aloud. Soon she too was asleep.

In Cherry Cottage, Lower Holtbury, Daphne had her bath. Afterwards she came downstairs, in her dressing gown, and turned on the television. There was nothing about the missing child on the late news. She made herself a cup of tea and wandered about, drinking it. What could Alan be doing, all this time? Was he still with that woman? She looked up Waring in the telephone directory, but there was no number for anyone of that name in Berbridge. Anyway, even if there had been, how could she ring up a woman whose child was missing at such a time? Why hadn't Alan rung her again?

At last she gave up and went to bed, but she could not sleep. Her mind raced round, puzzling about Alan. They'd always trusted one another; they had no secrets from each other. Or so she had thought.

Well, whatever happened, he'd have to go to the office on Monday. She'd break with practice and ring him up there, if he hadn't come home by then.

18

Mrs Duncan, on Sunday morning, was most surprised to discover the dirty state her baby son's pram was in. The wheels were all caked with mud and the bodywork was wet. The baby still had his morning nap in the pram, which in bad weather was placed in the garage by the open door so that he breathed in the fresh, if damp, air his mother thought would be good for him.

Their car had been very wet when they put it away the previous night. Mr Duncan said perhaps it was condensation. But condensation didn't explain the mud, pointed out his wife, and when she went to make up the pram with the mattress and bedding which were always taken into the house at night, she saw splinters of wood on the plastic lining. She puzzled about it, on and off, throughout Sunday morning. Surely the baby-sitter, the night before, hadn't taken the baby out somewhere?

Of course not, her husband said when she put forward this worrying theory. She must have pushed the pram through muddy puddles herself, and forgotten.

But the day before they'd gone out in the car. The pram hadn't been pushed out since Friday, and then it was only down to the shops and not to the recreation ground, where Mrs Duncan sometimes went when the weather was fine, on her way to the towpath. She liked to look at the river.

Dick and Bea Pearce, in Lower Holtbury, had people in for drinks on Sunday morning.

'Does anyone know what Alan's been up to?' Bea wanted to know, handing cheese straws. Daphne had rung that morning and made an excuse for their absence; Alan was getting a cold, she said, but her voice sounded odd; not like herself at all. Wouldn't she come on her own, Bea had suggested, and Daphne had refused, which was out of character. The Parkers were two who didn't live in each other's pockets.

The garage doors at Cherry Cottage were shut when Bea went past with the dog, but she hadn't forgotten the newspapers stuck in the letter-box while Daphne was away, and the milk on the step.

She mentioned these things to her Sunday guests.

'He can't have left home,' someone said. 'Not Alan.'

'Nor be having an affair,' someone else went on. 'Could he?'

A silence fell. Uneasy glances were exchanged, and the women moved closer to their husbands, for if Alan, that model, could stray, no one was safe.

In their separate bed-sitters, Sandra and Jenny rose early on Sunday morning to make their respective apple pie and lemon cheesecake. Intent and busy, they worked away, their doors open on the attic landing to keep them in touch with each other and with Sandra's radio on.

Terence Henshaw was laying the table in the ground

floor flat while Jean stuffed the pork. He'd already peeled the potatoes – quantities, as many as would fit in the roasting tin, for who knew what number would actually be in the house when lunch time came? A police car had driven up earlier, but brought no news; it was just a routine call to see how Louise had weathered the night. A journalist had rung the Henshaws' bell, and Terence had enjoyed telling him to get lost.

'We should ask Mrs Cox,' he said to Jean. 'There's plenty of food, after all. I bet she hasn't had a decent roast for years. Probably just pecks at a small chop on her own.'

Jean thought Mrs Cox looked quite well nourished, but she agreed with the sentiment.

'Yes, ask her, do,' she said.

Terence went downstairs at ten o'clock. He rang the bell at the basement flat and stood on the step, whistling. There was quite a delay, and he rang again. Then he heard a rather cross voice.

'Yes? Who's there?' Mrs Cox called sharply.

She had woken late, and her head was aching. All her muscles were sore and her back was stiff; she could not stand straight.

'Mrs Cox, it's Terence Henshaw, from upstairs. Can I have a word?' Terence called cheerily, moving from one foot to the other as he waited. It was cold and misty; the rain had stopped and every tree and shrub in the garden dripped with moisture.

There was the sound of bolts being drawn and the door opened. Mrs Cox peered round it. Her hair was disordered and her always pale face had a yellowish tinge. She looked really ill, Terence thought, in surprise.

'I just wanted to ask you to lunch,' he said. 'We're cooking some pork for everyone in the house – you know, because of the trouble upstairs – poor little Tessa.'

Mrs Cox had opened the door a little wider but Terence saw that she was barely taking in what he said. She wore a man's thick, woollen cardigan but she was shivering, and was almost unkempt when always, before, she'd appeared so neat.

'Will you come to lunch?' he repeated. 'In our flat upstairs?' and he beamed at her, adding, to tempt, 'Roast pork.'

'I'm not very well,' Mrs Cox said. She took her hand from the door and drew the cardigan more closely across her chest. 'Thank you, no,' she managed to add.

Terence's gaze, as she moved, left her face for an instant and went past her. It was gloomy inside the room. He felt curious. It must be depressing down here, all on her own, he thought. His eye caught a patch of something red on the floor and he focused on it, frowning.

'Won't you really?' he pressed. 'Please do.' He stared at the small red object, puzzled.

'No,' Mrs Cox was saying, moving to close the door.

'I'll bring your lunch down, then,' Terence spoke slowly to her now. 'I'll lay you a tray. I'll see you then.'

Before she had closed the door he had bounded up the basement steps and was haring round to the entrance to his own flat.

It was a little red glove which lay on the floor of Mrs Cox's living-room, under an upright chair. Terence raced past Jean, almost knocking her over in his hurry to get to the telephone. She heard him telling the police what he had seen.

Everyone knew that Tessa had worn her red gloves the day she had disappeared.

Chief Superintendent Drummer was in his office when Terence Henshaw's call came through, so he heard the news at once.

He went round to Oak Way himself, with a back-up car containing a uniformed sergeant and a woman police constable.

First, Drummer and the sergeant went to the Henshaws' ground floor flat, for a quick repeat of Terence's story, while the woman police constable stayed at the gate in case Mrs Cox sought to leave, though she could not see the police car, nor the two men, from her basement.

All three officers then went to Mrs Cox's door, and they took Terence with them.

151

'She'll open to you,' Drummer said. 'She may not want to let us come in.'

'Mrs Cox, Mrs Cox,' Terence called, after ringing the bell, which pealed sharply behind the black door. 'It's Terence Henshaw here, about your lunch.'

It was suddenly silent. The three police officers all stood against the wall so that if Mrs Cox looked out of the window she could not see them. Then they heard a shuffling sound.

'What's that?' came a cross-sounding voice from inside. 'It's not time yet.'

'It's about the pudding,' Terence said. 'Do you like apple pie? Please open the door, Mrs Cox.'

If she didn't, they'd soon break it in, he and the two coppers, both burly men, Terence thought. God, was that poor little kid in there, all the time?

The bolts slid back and the door opened a crack. Mrs Cox's pale face looked out.

'What's that you say?' she asked.

The next few seconds were a blur of movement. The door was pushed back, almost knocking Mrs Cox off her feet, and the policewoman slipped in to hold her arm. Terence stood by the door and pointed silently to where the glove still lay. It had dropped from Tessa's pocket when she took off her coat on Friday and hung it over a chair. Mrs Cox had done no cleaning since then, and had not seen it on the floor. When she put the child into her coat the night before, she had fastened only one toggle, and she had not noticed the slight bulge of the other glove in the pocket.

'Where is she? Where is Tessa, Mrs Cox?' Drummer asked.

Mrs Cox shook her head.

'I don't know,' she said. 'It's got nothing to do with me. I never saw her.'

Drummer and the sergeant went quickly through the flat. Tessa's satchel hung on a peg in the kitchen, where Mrs Cox had put it on Friday.

'What about this?' Drummer said, holding it up. It swung from his hand. 'Tessa took this to school on Friday.'

Mrs Cox began to mutter and sniffle.

'What's that?' Drummer snapped. 'Speak up, Mrs Cox. Tell us where Tessa is.'

'She ran off,' Mrs Cox said. 'She came in – on Friday. Then she ran off, when I was making the tea. Just ran away.' She rummaged in her cardigan pocket and took out a handkerchief, a large one, snowy white, and began snuffling into it.

'Why didn't you tell us this on Friday, Mrs Cox?' Drummer inquired. His tone was stern.

'I was frightened,' Mrs Cox said. 'I was afraid her mother would be angry with me. She's a strange woman, that,' she added, more strongly. Then she looked at Drummer defiantly, the handkerchief still in her hand. 'Tessa ran off because her mother wasn't there. She went looking for her, I expect.'

While this conversation went on, the sergeant had been going more thoroughly round the flat. He had lifted the lid of the chest in the room where they stood.

'Better come here a minute, sir,' he said in a very quiet voice.

Drummer went over and looked into the chest. The soft blanket inside was crushed as if a small body had lain upon it. There were indentations, like heel marks, in the fabric. The sergeant leaned in and pointed. A long, fair hair clung to the wool.

Drummer had expected to see the child's body inside the chest. This, at least, was a sort of reprieve.

'My God,' he said softly. 'Get the SOCO boys here at once.' He turned to Mrs Cox. 'Where is Tessa now, Mrs Cox?' he demanded. 'Are you going to tell me now, or would you prefer to come to the police station?' What had happened here? Had it been some strange game of hide-and-seek that somehow went wrong?

Mrs Cox stared at him, silently, her body stiff. The policewoman still held her arm.

'Well?' Drummer's expression was grim. This was a most unlikely child molester but Tessa had certainly been here, and lain in that chest. The Scenes-of-Crime Officer and his team would have to take the place apart, lift up the floor if necessary, if Mrs Cox would not make a full statement.

She looked back at him, sullen now, in a manner all too familiar to Drummer. This was no kind, retired pensioner; this was a villain.

'Very well,' he said shortly. 'The station it is. You'll tell me there. I've a feeling it won't be your first time inside a nick.'

He fetched her coat himself from the bedroom cupboard, treading gingerly in order not to disturb any evidence which there might be. He had no hope, now, of finding Tessa alive but as he glanced round the bedroom at the photographs on display, no bells rang in his mind. He'd been a young copper, still in the traffic division, when little Grace died all those years ago, murdered by her nanny.

19

Ruth had gone round to the Henshaws to discuss what to do about lunch, as Louise wouldn't agree to leave the flat in case there was news about Tessa. On the way past the basement flat to the front door entrance, she'd noticed activity down below.

'Why don't we bring your lunch up to you?' Jean Henshaw suggested. 'Your three helpings, I mean. It's what we intended to do for Mrs Cox, after all. Take it to her, I mean.'

'What is going on down there?' Ruth asked.

They couldn't have found Tessa, in spite of the glove, Jean thought, or Ruth wouldn't be here now. The police had sent Terence away as soon as they'd got into the basement flat. She told Ruth how he had noticed the glove on the floor below the chair.

'So she must have been there, in the flat,' Jean said. 'Terence said he heard Mrs Cox say she'd run off, but if that was true, why didn't she tell the police?'

'Do you think it's likely?' Ruth asked. 'Surely Tessa's too

154

sensible?' She remembered the terrible fright Louise had sustained at much the same age. 'Unless she was frightened,' she qualified. 'But how would Mrs Cox alarm her? Louise says she often went into the flat.'

'I think she did,' said Jean. 'They'd chat together in the garden. Mrs Cox has a way with children – she was a nanny, or something.'

'I'd better not mention this to Louise,' Ruth decided. 'The police will tell her as soon as there's anything definite.' There couldn't be good news, she thought, or that would have been relayed at once. The sense of dread, which she had been doing her best to suppress, rose in her again. 'Do bring us our lunch, please. It's very kind of you. Perhaps we'll be able to get Louise to eat something. At the moment she's making a cake. She thinks Tessa might be back for tea.'

'Oh dear,' said Jean. 'Do you?'

'I don't know what to think,' Ruth said. 'But it's giving her something to do.'

That morning, Alan had gone out to buy the Sunday papers. He'd passed a telephone box – the one from which, on Friday, Louise had called the police – and had thought about ringing Daphne, but what could he say to her? He couldn't explain in just a few words. It would have to be faced later, when he'd been able to think of what to say. She would have to know, in the end, about his loss of a job and about his involvement with Louise, for the one thing that mattered now was to support Louise through this horror at no matter what cost to his marriage. Daphne had friends; her work; her golf; while Louise had only Ruth Graham, it seemed, and himself, if Tessa was really lost for ever.

He did not go into the telephone box.

Louise made fudge, when she'd mixed the cake, and Alan and Ruth tried to read the newspapers. Now and then they read snippets out to each other, frivolous items. All the papers carried short reports about Tessa. At intervals one of them went to the kitchen to hover around Louise. Alan found her crying, tears rolling down her face as she beat her mixture. He said nothing, simply took her bowl from her and folded her into his arms. After a while she dried her eyes and went on with her self-imposed task.

Tessa had been having a nasty dream, about hide-and-seek and bad mummies. She tried very hard to wake up and call out for her own mummy, who was a good mummy and who'd been more smiley and cheerful lately, but her eyes wouldn't open.

She felt dreadfully sick. She seemed to remember being sick not long ago.

Retching, Tessa tried to sit up but her head bumped against something. She somehow managed to open her eyes as she fell back, but she was in total darkness. Tears sprang to her eyes – tears of terror and of discomfort, but her main awareness was of nausea. She put up a groping hand and felt some hard substance. Instinct made her push against it and it moved. Tessa pushed again, using both hands, and the wooden lid of the bunk base locker in which she lay yielded.

Pale light from the lamp of the towpath filtered into the cabin, past thin cotton curtains drawn over the windows. Tessa struggled to keep her eyes open, sitting up, blinking. She was in a small, confined space.

She retched again, and put a hand to her mouth. The jolting ride in the pram, over the recreation ground and along the towpath, followed by Mrs Cox's struggle to heave her on board the cabin cruiser moored near the bridge, had shaken her stomach up and provoked this rejection of the mixture of drugs she had consumed.

Mrs Cox had intended to dump the child's unconscious body in the water. She'd drown, then; and she wouldn't suffer, since she was fast asleep. Mrs Cox didn't like innocent children to suffer. She'd wheeled her load along the towpath looking for a suitable spot in an unlit area, but dense reeds at the riverside were something she hadn't foreseen. She could not throw Tessa far enough into the river to clear them. Seeking a gap, she came to the boat moored by the path and stopped, remembering that other boat so long ago.

Grace had been comfortable, sleeping there in the bunk,

just as Tessa had been comfortable in the chest in Mrs Cox's basement room, and then in Mavis's bed.

The river would be so cold, and that was bad for a child. She might wake and choke to death. Sleep was so peaceful.

Mrs Cox had propped the pram against a bollard so that, top-heavy as it was with the unconscious child inside, it would not tip up. She had peered through the rain and the gloom at the boat. A lamp nearby lit it dimly, and she saw that there was a mackintosh cover over the cockpit. Mrs Cox had taken her torch out of her holdall bag and shone it on the canopy which clipped round the cockpit, she saw, with the flap hanging loose at the bottom. She had unfastened enough of the cover to let her get into the cockpit.

The boat rocked under her weight as she moved on the narrow deck. It rocked more as she dragged Tessa, her hands under the child's arms, across the gap from the bank to the deck and down into the well of the cockpit. It was not easy to do, but Mrs Cox was still strong. She played her torch on the cabin door. It was locked. That other boat had been open.

She could have left Tessa in the cockpit and fastened the canopy again, but it was cold out there, and damp. A child should always be kept warm and dry. Mrs Cox, friend of Mavis who had been a thief, had looked at the lock and thought it should be easy to break. She'd need to use something heavy – her shoe might do, or her torch, she'd thought. Bending down, she had peered about on the floor of the cockpit and saw, tucked under a thwart, a strong metal bar, the boat's mooring spike. It was just the thing; a few blows and the job was done.

The boat's interior was not very different from that of *The Happy Maid*. Mrs Cox found a locker beneath a berth, and placed the child inside. This time, there were no life-jackets to form a mattress, but there was an oilskin which would cushion Tessa. Mrs Cox had lifted her into the locker and arranged her neatly, hands by her sides. Using the finger holes drilled in the top, she replaced the lid. There were no cushions, for the owner had taken them into his house for the winter. Mrs Cox had closed the cabin door and had refastened the sides of the canopy when she left. The river

157

area had already been searched, she knew. The police would not be back, or not until it was much too late to save Tessa's life. She would not be found until the boat's owner opened his locker, Mrs Cox had thought as she wheeled the empty pram away.

Tessa's extreme nausea made her ignore the bruises she had sustained being dragged on board as she clambered out of the locker. Because she had so often been aboard Dick Tremayne's boat at Portrinnock, she was somehow aware, now, subconsciously, that she was in a boat, and this helped to contain her panic as she blundered about in the faint light that came from the lamp on the bank outside, seeking a place to be tidily sick.

She didn't quite make the small lavatory, but she had stumbled out of the main cabin, through the dividing curtain, before she vomited. She felt very cold and shaky afterwards, and tears flowed as she hugged her arms to her chest, gasping and shuddering.

As she stood, doubled over, she remembered about Mummy. Mrs Cox had said they were going to see her. Why was she in a boat? Were they going by sea to London? The boat didn't seem to be moving, and where was Mrs Cox? Tessa called her, in a quavery voice, but there was no answer.

Moving very slowly, she returned to the main cabin. She was shivering, her teeth chattering. It was a very great effort to climb on a bunk and look out of the window. Tessa still felt very confused and sleepy as she peered out and saw land. Perhaps they were at an island?

She was so cold!

Tessa felt in her pockets for her gloves but could only find one, and that made her cry still more, for she loved her red gloves which Mummy had made her for Christmas. She put it on and pulled her cap down over her ears. Then because it was still night, and at night you slept, she climbed back into her box-like bed, leaving the lid open and drawing the heavy oilskin round her.

Crying weakly, coughing a little, sore from her vomiting and still feeling the effects of the drugs – but no longer retaining a fatal dose – Tessa fell asleep once more.

At midnight, the lamp on the towpath went out.

It was daylight when she woke again. Her mouth felt peculiar and her head ached. For a while she kept drowsing off and then waking. She heard the lap of the water against the side of the boat; it was a nice sound. Had she somehow been magicked on to Dick's boat? It was the only boat she knew. She lay there, the heavy oilskin over her, while she tried to puzzle it out.

Gradually, she remembered. There was something about naughty mummies that nagged at the edge of her mind. It was Daddy, though, not Mummy, who was naughty. He went away for days and days, and then, when he came home, scolded Mummy and made her cry. He was in heaven now, with Jesus, Tessa recalled.

But Mummy – something was wrong about Mummy.

Tessa was shocked fully awake when she remembered. Waves of terror swept over her, and she wept among her oilskins. She cried for a long time, but at last her sobs diminished from sheer exhaustion, and as they lessened she realized that she was alone, for when you cried, in the end someone came.

She climbed heavily out of the locker, aware, now, of her various aches and bruises. There was a horrid taste in her mouth and she was dreadfully thirsty. She stood in the narrow alley by the bunk and stared about her in the pale morning light.

This wasn't Dick's boat. His had a small, separate galley with two burners and a tiny sink. This boat was bigger, and had a proper cooker. There was a sink beside it, and where there were taps, there was water. Tessa turned the tap and a trickle ran out. She looked about for a mug, and found one in a cupboard. She filled it and drank it straight down, then filled it again and drank the second mugful more slowly. She felt better after that, and when she had rinsed the cup and set it upside down on the drainer to dry, she looked in the other cupboards round the sink. Some were too high for her to reach, but she found a bucket and stood on that. Her reward was to find a toothbrush. She hoped the owner wouldn't mind if, just this once, she used it.

Tessa brushed her teeth hard, spitting vigorously. She

felt much better after that, except that all of a sudden she was very hungry. She searched through the cupboards. Perhaps there would be some cornflakes. It must be breakfast time by now.

At this thought, tears flowed again, for breakfast was always a happy time in the kitchen with Mummy, milk in the blue and white jug, her own bowl with her name on the rim, and sometimes honey.

But she was going to see Mummy in hospital in London. Mrs Cox was taking her but had somehow vanished, so Tessa must just carry on by herself – have breakfast first, and then look for someone else on this island where the boat was moored, who would show her the way to London. Once in London, she'd ask the way to the hospital; anyone in London would know where the hospital was.

There were some tins of soup and a can of beer in the galley cupboard, and a few very damp, soggy digestive biscuits at the end of a packet.

Tessa could cook some soup, if there were matches. She wasn't allowed to light them unless Mummy was there, but this was an emergency; she knew that word; it was one her father had often used.

She found a box of matches in a drawer, and a tin opener, the kind you stab into the tin and then make walk round the edge; she had seen her mother use one like that on picnics. She couldn't work it properly, but she made a few holes in the top of the tin and managed to get most of the soup out through them, though she cut her hand slightly and left a smear of blood on the drainer. She sucked at the wound, which was trivial.

When she found the gas wouldn't light, she wept again, but after a short burst of sobs, remembered once more what went on in Dick's boat. The gas came from a big cylinder and had to be turned on and off when you came aboard and left. She found the cylinder forward in the boat, passing a nasty mess of sick on the floor. It smelled horrid, making Tessa retch again, and sharply reminding her of what memory had blotted out; that it was she who had been sick here, in the night.

She felt ashamed. She'd have to clear up the awful mess,

but first she must turn on the cylinder. Tessa grasped the knob on the top. It was very stiff, but at last, using both hands, she managed to move it.

She lit the gas and heated her lumpy soup. It was only lukewarm when she ate it, but she crumbled some digestive biscuits into it and tipped it into a yellow plastic bowl. There was a spoon to use. It was quite a nice breakfast, really, Tessa thought, washing the bowl and the pan in cold water from the tap and not noticing that her efforts were only partly successful.

Now she must explore. She pulled her red woollen hat securely around her ears and fastened her coat. She put on her one glove. Then she opened the cabin door, to find the cockpit enclosed by the canvas canopy.

She'd never seen one of those on Dick's boat. It would stop her from landing on the island, which she could see through the perspex panel. She beat against it, crying again, and then saw that it hung quite loose.

Tessa wriggled through, under the flap, on to the narrow deck. Land was near, and she jumped.

It was sheer chance that she turned, on the bank, to the left and not to the right, and so, before long, found herself by the recreation ground. Even then, in the mist, with the trees dripping in the still air, she instinctively followed the path to the gate because it led away from the water and did not recognize where she was at first. She was still sobbing a little as her legs carried her in the right direction, along Shippham Avenue.

She thought of the dragon, then, on the corner. In the mist he could pounce without her seeing. Tessa ran past his bush and into Oak Way before he could snap her up.

She must get to Mummy. Mrs Cox had said she would take her. Somehow she must have left the boat and gone back to her own flat. Tessa hurried to find her.

When she saw Alan's car in the road, her heart leaped. Alan would take her to Mummy. She hastened on, walking as fast as she could.

There were other cars outside the house, too; white ones. Tessa did not recognize them as police cars; she was too intent on reaching home; but she was rather surprised to find a very tall policeman standing just inside the gateway of number 51. He was occupying his dull vigil by inspecting a viburnum growing there as he protected the place from the curious, lest news that Mrs Cox had been taken to Berbridge Central Police Station should leak out.

He stared at the small intruder, then bent down to gaze at her incredulously.

Tessa's face, beneath her woolly cap, was dirty and tear-stained, but it was also unmistakably the face in the photograph of the missing child.

'I want my mummy,' Tessa said, lower lip quivering.

'Come along then, Tessa,' said the constable, and took her hand. He led her past the steps leading down to the basement, which his colleagues were busy examining, and walked her up the steps to her mother's flat.

'I've got my key,' Tessa said, and with the hand that was not clasping his, began to fish for it round her neck.

'That's all right, Tessa,' the constable said, and cleared his throat in which a large lump seemed to have suddenly risen. 'Mummy's at home, waiting for you,' and he pressed the bell hard.

A lady in a dark skirt and jacket, whom Tessa had never seen before, opened the door.

'Here's somebody who wants her mummy,' said the constable, and the startled policewoman stepped back, holding the door wide.

The flat seemed to be full of people. Alan was there, and Mr and Mrs Henshaw from downstairs, and Ruth, but Tessa had no time to wonder why; her one thought was to get to her mother, who was sitting in her usual corner of the sofa and not wrapped up in bandages, as Tessa had expected.

For an instant no one in the room moved, staring in disbelief at the small grubby figure standing in the doorway holding the tall police constable's hand. Then Louise sprang forward at the same moment that Tessa let go of the policeman, and they rushed towards each other, both of them bursting into tears of exhausted relief as Louise fell on her knees to clasp Tessa in her arms.

20

'Mrs Cox said we were going to see you at London,' said Tessa, when the first commotion had died down. 'We went in a boat. She said you'd been run over, Mummy. Didn't you look carefully before crossing the road?'

Louise could not answer; her throat was choked with tears as she held Tessa close.

Tessa's eye was caught by a plate of biscuits on the table.

'I'm hungry,' she said. 'Can I have a biscuit?'

Chief Superintendent Drummer came in while she was still eating it.

'Hullo, Tessa,' he said. 'So you got lost, did you?'

'I thought it was a desert island,' said Tessa.

'Where was that?' Drummer asked in a matter-of-fact voice, sitting down and taking a biscuit himself.

'Where the boat landed, of course,' Tessa said.

'The boat?' Drummer asked. 'Were you on a boat?'

'Mm. It wasn't the same as Dick's,' Tessa said. 'There weren't any sails. There was soup. Oh!' and she put her hand to her mouth in dismay. 'I forgot,' she said, and her lip trembled. She began to whimper.

'Forgot what?' Louise asked, hugging her. She felt she would never be able to let her out of her sight again.

'To clean up,' Tessa whispered, hiding her face. 'I was sick.'

'That doesn't matter, darling,' Louise said. 'It was an accident.'

Drummer was beaming. Find the vomit, he thought, and the lab would be able to say if it contained drugs. The evidence found in the basement flat – the drugs in the bathroom cupboard and the sediment in a glass in the bedroom – might tie up the case against Mrs Cox, though how had she managed to take the child, unobserved, from her flat to a boat? He saw that Tessa had cut her hand;

dried blood was mingled with dirt. There would be traces of Tessa left in the boat, just as there were in the basement flat – blood possibly, maybe another long fair hair or some thread from her clothing. And Mrs Cox, herself, might have left proof of her presence.

'I forgot to turn off the gas too,' Tessa was saying. 'Dick always turns his off.'

'We'll see to it, Tessa,' said Drummer. 'Don't you worry. Where was the boat? How did you get there?'

'I don't remember,' Tessa frowned. 'I just remember you weren't here, Mummy, and Mrs Cox came.'

'Was the boat far away, Tessa?' Drummer asked. He knew the boats by the river had been inspected when Tessa was first missed; how had she not been found then? She'd been concealed in the flat at first; that was certain, but for how long?

'It was near the rec,' Tessa said. 'It wasn't an island after all. There were nice pink curtains.'

The pattern, though modified, repeated, Drummer thought grimly. In the basement flat, Mrs Cox's newspaper cuttings had been discovered and the police knew that they had in their charge a convicted child murderer who, after serving her time in prison, had made a new life in Berbridge under another name. The scenes-of-crime team examining the flat had found a Mars Bar, wrapped in a handkerchief, tucked down the side of the wing armchair; it bore the clear impression of a child's teeth and had been sent to the lab for testing. Some providential chance had caused Tessa to bring up the drugs she had swallowed, and saved her from inhaling her vomit. Her life had been preserved by luck, he thought.

In the background, Ruth and the woman police constable were murmuring about taking Tessa to hospital, but the child seemed quite well and alert. Only Drummer, of the company, knew that she had probably ingested a large dose of drugs, and even WPC Frost did not yet know Mrs Cox's true identity. Louise, clutching the child, shook her head when she caught the drift of the discussion.

'It would be like what happened to me all over again,' she kept saying.

164

Drummer did not understand what she meant but he did not press Louise. Instead, from the Henshaws' flat, he telephoned her doctor, who was off duty. His partner, a woman, agreed to come round at once and it was decided that she should be the judge of whether Tessa need be taken to hospital.

The doctor was gentle and kind, and said that she thought home, her mother, rest and warmth were the best medicines now for Tessa. The bruises on Tessa's legs and body were not, she thought, due to blows but were knocks of a lesser kind. Her reflexes were normal.

'Were you very sick?' she asked Tessa.

'Very,' Tessa confirmed. 'And in Mrs Cox's bathroom, too.'

The doctor conferred with Drummer, who told her what had been found in the basement flat. Tessa had probably been given nitrazepam, he said, and perhaps a baby sedative. Chloral hydrate had been found, too. These drugs, said the doctor, were, it could generally be said, fatal only in large doses. Chloral hydrate was an irritant and could be corrosive; it tasted very bitter. She couldn't be certain without looking it up, but she had an idea it interacted with antihistamine, the main ingredient of the baby sedative, and so would provoke nausea. These circumstances had combined to save Tessa.

There had been no sodium amytal handy this time, Drummer thought grimly; Tessa would not have recovered from that, any more than the other child so long ago.

The doctor said she would return later in the day to make sure Tessa was not in need of more treatment, and advised a bland diet with plenty of fluid. When she and Drummer were gone, Tessa had a bath and a hairwash, and dressed in clean clothes. WPC Frost took away what she had worn during her captivity, each garment sealed in a plastic bag, for traces from Mrs Cox's person or clothing might be found on them by the lab.

After that, everyone went down to lunch in the Henshaw's flat, which Tessa thought was quite an excitement. Mrs Henshaw had come to the door and talked to Mummy and then they'd all gone round the house and through the front entrance to the big ground floor flat, with Tessa wearing a padded anorak of Mummy's since the police had gone off with her own coat and Mummy said she mustn't catch cold after her bath. The anorak hung down past her hands and reached to her ankles.

Tessa had scrambled egg for lunch, instead of roast pork – the pork smelled good, but somehow she didn't want any. After that, she had lots of ice cream. She still didn't understand why Mrs Cox had told such a fib about Mummy, who hadn't been hurt at all, but had just missed her train. It all seemed a bit puzzling, but everything was all right now. Unlike someone older, Tessa required no explanation for Ruth's unexpected presence.

Drummer returned in the afternoon to tell Louise what had been discovered. The Henshaws had known that Mrs Cox went baby-sitting regularly, and the police had found a diary in her kitchen, with 'Bradley, 7 p.m.', entered for Saturday. They had soon traced the Bradleys, just round the corner in Shippham Avenue. Mrs Bradley had been rather surprised, this morning, to find on the kitchen cork tiles, beside the boiler, a stain such as a very wet raincoat might leave if it was hung nearby and dripped. She'd cleaned off the mark, but the policeman who had called to inquire whether Mrs Cox had kept her appointment could take her word that it had been there. Her husband had fetched Mrs Cox by car, she said, and had taken her home later – about midnight, she added.

The constable went next door, as routine, to ask if the neighbours had noticed anything odd the previous evening. There, he was shown the pram, still muddy, though the worst of the dirt had been wiped off. The lab could analyse what was left to see if it matched that in the recreation ground or on the river bank. They'd seek other proof of how the pram had been used; there would be traces.

The boat with the pink curtains was soon found, with the broken lock on the cabin door. Detectives were now painstakingly examining it for evidence to prove that Mrs Cox had been there.

In Berbridge Central Police Station, Mrs Cox raved insanely when challenged by Drummer. At first she had refused to talk at all; then she had begun to cry and talk about wickedness stalking the earth, waiting for little girls who must be saved from evil. After that, suddenly, she snapped, all reason lost. Drummer thought she might never be fit to come to trial, but she would certainly not be free to threaten the safety of anyone ever again.

After Tessa's return, Ruth had telephoned Freda. She rang again in the afternoon, to say she would be leaving for Cornwall soon, and should be back between nine and ten that night. She came back from this second call looking thoughtful. The others were about to have tea, settled cosily round the gas fire in the sitting-room. Tessa was preparing to cut the cake, an orange sponge, which Louise had made that morning.

'How would you feel about coming back to Portrinnock, Louise?' Ruth asked, when this important task was complete.

Tessa, her slice of cake in her hand, paused with it in the air and caught her breath. She looked at her mother.

'For a holiday?' Louise was saying.

'No,' said Ruth. 'For good. Marjorie Browne – the receptionist,' she added to Alan, 'is pregnant. She wants to leave in the summer and her job will be going. Your mother suggested you might like it.'

'She did?' Louise clasped her hands together. 'You're telling the truth, Ruth? It wasn't your idea?'

'No, I promise,' said Ruth. 'She asked me to tell you.'

Tessa's eyes were shining. There was no doubt what she thought about such a plan.

Ruth's gaze held Louise's, across the room.

'It's your decision, Louise,' she emphasized. 'Yours alone – no one else's,' and she nodded meaningly in Tessa's direction. 'You couldn't live at the hotel, there isn't room, but you could find a flat or cottage to rent in Portrinnock, I'm sure. Don't decide now – take time to think it over.' She cut a sliver of cake and held it, ready to eat. 'Why not come down when Tessa's term ends and see how you feel then? You could ask about the school and so on.' She popped the piece of cake into her mouth. 'Delicious,' she said, and added, to Alan, 'The present receptionist lives in the town and comes in every day.'

Tessa had forgotten about the cake.

'Oh, Mummy!' she breathed.

They would go, Alan knew with bleak foreboding. It would be right for them both. Louise had ghosts from the past to lay and she needed to come to terms with her mother. Perhaps her gremlin attacks were cured, but she might, he feared, have more. If so, in the more tranquil, slower-living West Country she would find it easier to cope with them. What could he, after all, offer her that could compare with the security her mother, and the thriving hotel, would provide? He had no job; he was married; he was much older than she was.

He looked stricken, Ruth saw. Would he try to persuade Louise not to accept her mother's offer?

Alan sipped his tea. Nothing would alter at once. Louise needed him now while she recovered from these last terrible days, and he must help her to find her own way to a decision without letting her see that he would be desolate without her. He would never forget this brief love, but he must let her go when she was ready.

There was this fellow, Dick, whoever he was, with his boat, in Portrinnock. Louise had known him for years. Was he married?

Alan plodded through a slice of cake while they talked about her mother's suggestion.

'You should think about it, Louise, as Ruth says,' he advised.

Before Ruth left, he went round to the Henshaws' flat to telephone Daphne. It couldn't be postponed any longer. Their telephone was attached to the kitchen wall, and they tactfully closed the door so that he could talk privately.

'Tessa's been found,' he said.

'I know,' Daphne said. 'It was on the one o'clock news.'

'She's quite all right,' Alan continued. 'Not hurt, I mean.'

'Yes. So it said on the radio,' Daphne replied. No other details had been given; Daphne knew nothing about Mrs Cox and her part in Tessa's disappearance. 'You'll be home soon, then,' she said.

168

'No.' Alan could dodge it no longer. He plunged. 'I can't leave Louise now,' he said. 'She's had the most dreadful shock. I'm staying.'

Daphne heard the words, but she would not accept their message.

'You mean you'll be going straight to the office from there in the morning?' she said.

She still didn't know! So much had happened in the last hours that this fact had been driven from Alan's mind.

'No,' he said again.

'What do you mean? Are you taking the day off?'

'I haven't been near the office for weeks,' Alan said. 'I was sacked – made redundant.'

'Oh!' Daphne's voice came as a wail. 'Oh, Alan,' she cried. Her mind was reeling. 'She's not your secretary then? This girl – what's her name?'

'Louise,' Alan said. 'No, she's not.'

'You said she was,' Daphne accused. 'You lied to me, Alan.'

'Yes,' he admitted, but Daphne was rushing on.

'Why didn't you tell me you'd been sacked?' she asked.

'I tried, Daphne, but you wouldn't listen,' he said. She wasn't listening now, not to what he was really trying to say. 'We can't discuss it on the phone,' he went on. 'There's a lot I've got to explain, but I'm afraid it must wait.'

'But your job, Alan,' Daphne said. 'What are you doing about finding another?'

'I'm looking,' he said. 'I'll tell you about it later. I can't stop now. I'll ring you tomorrow.'

It was her hospital day tomorrow, he remembered. He might be able to postpone explaining until the dust had time to settle. He'd ring in the morning and make sure she had left as usual, then go round to pick up some clothes. He was moving in with Louise until he was sure she could manage without him – until she wanted him to go.

At last Daphne understood what he was saying. He meant to spend the night with that girl.

'You must come home, Alan,' she said. 'Come home now.'

169

'I've told you already, Daphne, I can't leave Louise,' he said.

'But what about me?' Daphne said. 'I'm your wife!'

'I know, and I'm sorry to hurt you,' said Alan. 'I'm afraid I'm letting you down very badly.' He'd been weak and craven, he thought, and he shouldn't be doing this to Daphne at all, much less over the telephone. But he did not intend to let Louise down too: everyone else, except possibly Ruth, had failed her before, and if she was to face the future with courage, she must know that she could rely on him now. 'I'm needed here,' he said.

For a while, he thought, just a while; and he wondered if Daphne had ever really needed him.

'I'll ring tomorrow,' he said again. Perhaps they could talk in the evening, if she wasn't off at bridge or badminton.

Daphne replaced the receiver without replying. She stood staring at it, eyes smarting, but her tears were of anger, not grief.

How dare he behave like this! It was some sort of middle-aged madness, of course. He'd return to his senses soon enough and come running back. Either that, or this girl would get tired of him. She must be feckless to let her child get lost, but if that hadn't happened, how long would it have been, Daphne wondered, before she found out what was going on?

To lose his job and not tell her! The enormity of it was shocking. Unless he soon found another, how could they continue to live at Cherry Cottage?

Daphne's world rocked. She would never give up her home. Nothing – no mad infatuation of Alan's – would be allowed to destroy her life, she decided grimly, already beginning to stitch up the great, ugly, gaping wound she would never acknowledge, either to herself or to anyone else. He would find a job, and a good one, and their life would resume, just as before. She would think of an excuse to explain his absence from home – a business trip abroad, perhaps. Meanwhile, she would not let her mind dwell on where Alan was now, or all it implied.

He would return.